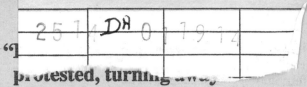
"I _____ protested, turning away ___

"No, that's not quite true. You don't *want* to love me anymore. There's a difference." Michael put his hands on her shoulders and she trembled at his touch.

"Let's make love and see what happens," he whispered in her ear. "It's the quickest way to find out how we really feel."

"You're a bastard, Michael," she said as her heart tripped faster and faster. "A first-class bastard."

"I've got to know," he replied, turning her to face him. "And I think you do, too."

Words of protest formed on her lips, but he kissed them away. He slipped his hand inside the opening of her robe, cupping one breast, and her resistance crumbled. The intervening years faded from memory.

They would make love....

Janice Kaiser has always been fascinated by Hollywood, the setting of her latest sizzling Temptation romance, *Star*. The movie capital is full of wonderful characters and their stories, she asserts. This talented writer is also part of a new project with Harlequin—Mira Books. *Private Sins,* a mainstream book written by Janice, will be available from Mira Books in March 1995. Look for it at your local bookstore!

Books by Janice Kaiser

HARLEQUIN TEMPTATION
444—FLYBOY
462—BETRAYAL
466—DECEPTIONS
477—WILD LIKE THE WIND

HARLEQUIN SUPERROMANCE
494—THE BIG SECRET
541—CRADLE OF DREAMS
597—THE YANQUI PRINCE

STAR
JANICE KAISER

Harlequin Books

TORONTO • NEW YORK • LONDON
AMSTERDAM • PARIS • SYDNEY • HAMBURG
STOCKHOLM • ATHENS • TOKYO • MILAN
MADRID • WARSAW • BUDAPEST • AUCKLAND

For Laurie Cahill

ISBN 0-373-25608-6

STAR

Copyright © 1994 by Belle Lettres, Inc.

Prologue

MICHAEL DREW HIS tongue up the underside of her breast. She tensed, struggling not to move. Then he pursed his lips, curved them around her nipple, and sucked hard. Her resolve crumbled. She moaned, clutching the sheet in her fists.

Michael did that to her. All he had to do was touch her and she was on the edge, ready to come. He virtually owned her body and she'd been foolish enough to tell him so. He had taken full advantage of that knowledge—as often as he could.

"I feel like a volcano ready to erupt," she murmured. "You'd better stop."

"Oh, but I want you to erupt," he whispered. "It's my favorite pastime, seeing you lose control. I plan to spend my whole life watching you doing it."

"You're a bastard, Michael Cross," she said, blushing. "You know that, don't you?"

"Uh-huh."

She listened to the rain drumming softly on the skylight of her little loft apartment. Alone she would listen to the pitter-patter by the hour—the sound of a thousand fingertips on glass—as well as the bellow of the tugs and ferries on Puget Sound. But with Michael flicking his tongue down her stomach, swirling it around her belly button before plunging it in, she could think of nothing but him and her desire. She felt herself start to pulse.

"You really have to stop now," she insisted.

"Why?"

"Because I don't want to come this way," she said. "Give me a minute to cool down. Please."

"Shall I get an ice cube? That might help you cool down."

"No!"

He laughed and propped himself up on his elbow. He admired her body in the candlelight. Michael loved candles and so did she. Theater was important to them, which was hardly surprising, and they found mutual delight in bringing it into their lovemaking. He took her hand and kissed her fingers.

Sometimes, when he was moved, he would recite lines from Shakespeare, especially *Romeo and Juliet*. He claimed that was entirely fitting and appropriate. She'd asked if he expected their love life to end so tragically. "Only onstage," he'd replied, "but not in bed. In bed it will never end." She'd laughed when he said that, but he insisted he was serious.

Michael Cross was a wonderful actor. Dina had learned so much from him already. Her own skills were not nearly so remarkable. Still, Michael had never quite gained the popularity that those who really knew his work believed he deserved. She, on the other hand, had been lucky, especially considering she'd been in the business for less than a third the time. "You were born under a lucky star," he'd told her.

Dina had asked if that was why he wanted to marry her—so that a little of her luck would rub off. "Yes," he'd replied. "I intend to exploit my marriage to you to the fullest."

As she lay naked on her bed, Michael drew his finger over the curve of her hip. She stared into his ultra-pale blue eyes, shining in the flickering candlelight. He stroked her hip, reciting lines from Shakespeare. But Dina didn't listen. She was more interested in his touch than his words.

"You're not paying attention to me," he said.

"Othello," she said, smiling at him. "So which am I, Desdemona or Juliet?"

"You know better than I, my love."

Michael rolled onto his back, putting his hand lovingly on her thigh as he gazed up at the vaulted ceiling and blackened skylight. "I dream my dreams, for it is meant that I would dream them for us both."

"A Midsummer Night's Dream?"

"No, just me," he said. "On a rainy night in Seattle, lying in bed beside my one true love." He turned his head toward her and smiled.

Dina tousled his blondish hair. "You silly goose."

Michael took her hand and stuck her little finger into his mouth, sucking on it as he had her nipple. Again she shivered.

"You've just got to keep me on edge, don't you?" she teased. "You refuse to let me have my body as my own."

"Your body's mine, my love. All mine."

"You can forget that!" she said, teasingly punching his shoulder.

Dina then turned onto her side, propped her head on her arm, and looked into his eyes. "Michael, I worry sometimes that we're approaching this marriage as though it's another production we're mounting."

His expression turned serious. "*We're* approaching the marriage this way, or *I'm* approaching it this way?"

She took his hand and rubbed the back of it against her cheek. "I'm really not accusing you of anything," she said. "Marriage is serious. I guess I'm just scared."

He studied her for a long moment. "There's no rush, Dina," he told her. "If you're feeling uncomfortable, we can delay things. Your mother and my brother are the only ones coming any distance. It's not like we've invested thousands of dollars in this particular date. A few hundred bucks is all that's at stake financially."

"No," she countered, kissing his knuckles. "I'm not saying I want to delay the wedding. And I'm definitely not having second thoughts. I don't want you to think that for a minute."

"Then what are you saying?"

She stared down at his hand. "Honestly?"

"Sure," he said with a laugh. "It's better than dishonestly."

"I'm scared, Michael. I'm scared that at times you romanticize me too much, that you aren't being realistic. I'm afraid you're making me into something I'm not."

He pushed her ebony hair back off her cheek. "I'm not under the illusion that you're perfect, honey. God knows, neither of us is."

"That's not what I mean."

"What *do* you mean?"

"What are you going to do when the bloom wears off your love for me?" she asked.

"It won't."

"Of course it will. People don't go on loving each other this way into their eighties. Love changes."

"Then I'll love you the way I will. I'm not worried about it."

She said nothing, though she wondered if Michael wasn't being naive. He could be such a romantic, and seemed blinded by passion at times.

"Evidently you are worried," he said.

"It's not what you're thinking, Michael."

"Do you really know what I'm thinking?"

"You think it's my feelings for you, but it isn't. I feel like it's opening night and I'm about to go out onto the stage in my first big role. I feel confident, but deep down I'm afraid I don't have what it takes to make the audience love me—not the way I want to be loved."

"You know, I'm not sure if we're talking about my feelings or yours."

She laughed. "You won't believe this, but I'm talking more about yours than mine."

He cupped her face in his hands, gently caressing her jaw. "When we came here from New York, I was afraid. I knew I was taking a big step. I was leaving a secure place at the bottom of the scale of actors who work regularly. But I also knew it wasn't that much to lose. Still, taking a risk isn't easy. And it wasn't easy to sign that lease on the warehouse. I knew that in starting a new theater I was putting my talent and skill—not to mention my modest fortune—on the line and risking failure. But I've never once had second thoughts about you, Dina. Maybe that tells you how naive I am, but it's absolutely true."

"I've been scared about the theater, too," she said. "I know what a risk you're taking. I admire you for your courage, Michael. I truly do."

"I wish you admired me for my good judgment when it comes to women," he said with a grin.

"But will you love me when I'm old and gray?"

"Yes," he replied, kissing the end of her nose. "As long as you don't lose your acting skills."

She gave him a playful punch. The telephone on the nightstand rang. They both looked at it.

Michael glanced at the clock. "Who could possibly be calling at this time of night?"

"I have no idea," she said.

"Well, my sweet, shall I answer it, or would a man's voice be too much of an embarrassment at eleven at night?"

"Don't be silly," she said, getting up. "Mom knows you sleep here more than you do at your place."

"And doesn't like it one little bit."

Dina reached for the phone. "My mother adores you, Michael Cross." She picked up the receiver. "Hello?"

"Dina," came a woman's voice, "did I wake you? Am I calling too late?"

It was Kit Mosley, her friend who'd gone right to Hollywood from the actors' workshop in New York where they'd both studied. "No, Kit. Michael and I were just talking." She gave him a wink. "What's up?"

"Sit down, Dina," her friend said, "if you aren't already."

"Why, Kit? What's happened?"

"Barry Stewart wants you to do a screen test for a part in his new film, *Sitting Pretty!*" Kit enthused. "Can you believe it?"

"Kit, you're kidding!"

"It's just a supporting role, but a damned good one. It's not a bit part."

"He liked the video, then?"

"He *loved* it! He said he definitely, absolutely, had to see more of you."

"When?"

"Like immediately, girl. Yesterday. Tomorrow at the latest."

"Kit, I'm getting married on Saturday."

There was a silence.

"Barry's casting the part on Friday. Shooting starts Monday," Kit said. "Carole Brenner turned up pregnant and thought she could get by with carefully chosen camera angles. Barry was livid. He tossed her out, but said he's got to have that look. He said it could be you."

Dina glanced at Michael, anxiety rising up in her. It was clear that he was totally perplexed by the conversation. She sighed woefully. "Kit, can I call you back in a few minutes?"

"I guess so. Sure."

"Are you at home?"

"Yeah."

"Give me ten minutes." She hung up the phone.

Michael was lying on his stomach, staring at her. For a moment neither of them said anything.

"That was Hollywood calling, wasn't it?" he said.

She nodded. "Yes. It was Kit. She's in a Barry Stewart film called *Sitting Pretty* that started shooting this week.

One of the actresses had to drop out at the eleventh hour and Kit told Barry about me. I'm the right type for the character, apparently. I haven't seen the script, but that's what Kit told me."

He gave her a calculating look. "Kind of strange that Barry Stewart should think of a stage actress in Seattle for a key role in a film, isn't it, Geraldine? Even if you happen to know Kit Mosley."

Michael always called her Geraldine when he was irritated. Back home in Cedar Rapids she'd been Geraldine Winterhalter, and still was, legally, though she'd used Dina Winters as her stage name since she'd first gone to New York.

"Kit showed him an old video that she and I did at the actors' workshop," she told Michael. "It seems he was impressed."

"Kit's sleeping with the sonofabitch," Michael said, sitting up, "so I'm sure he buys anything and everything she tells him."

"I know you don't like Kit, but she did me a big favor—something she didn't have to do. And I can't help but be flattered that Barry Stewart wants to test me."

"Well, let's just hope he isn't into ménages à trois."

"Michael! What a terrible thing to say! This has nothing to do with sex. It's work."

"Just like that? Out of the clear blue they want you for a screen test in Hollywood? I may be a dumb actor, Dina, but I'm no fool!"

"Michael, why are you getting upset about this? I thought you'd be pleased for me."

"Tell me the truth. How long have you been working on this, Dina?"

"Kit called me for the first time about it a week ago."

"Funny I never heard anything about it until now."

"I didn't see any point in making a big deal of it when I didn't expect anything to come of it. To be honest, I'd almost forgotten Kit called."

"Well, I can see how you wouldn't want to upset the apple cart. As things stand, there's a fifty-fifty chance you'll be marrying me next weekend. No point in announcing prematurely you've had a slight career adjustment that might interfere with the wedding, especially since you might not get the part."

Dina shook her head. "I can't believe this! You're furious because somebody wants to give me a screen test."

"Tell me, Geraldine, do we delay the ceremony so as not to interfere, or do you go down to L.A. instead of going on our honeymoon? I mean, it probably would be a good idea to do a little planning. It is, after all, our lives we're talking about."

Dina felt her own anger rise. "Michael, I haven't committed to anything. Obviously, I had to talk to you first, which is what I'm doing now. Unfortunately, you've assumed the worst and refuse to give me the benefit of the doubt."

"I'm not assuming anything," he replied. "I'm going strictly by what I hear. And I've got to tell you, as your *would-be* husband, I don't particularly like what I've heard."

"What do you mean, 'would-be'?" she retorted. "Are you trying to tell me something? Are you saying you'd rather call off the wedding than sit down and discuss our future like reasonable adults?"

"Oh, so it's our future we're discussing. We've jumped from a screen test to stardom already. Isn't there an intermediate step you've forgotten, Dina? Like getting the part, maybe?"

She picked up her robe from the chair and slipped it on, tying it securely around her waist. Then she stood glaring at him. "It pains me to say this, Michael, but I know what the problem is. You're jealous."

"What?"

"That's right, you're jealous. This doesn't have anything to do with our wedding, or our marriage. It has to do with your ego. You can't stand the thought that I may have an opportunity to take a big step in my career."

"Well, at least we're getting to the point. *Egos*. Please note I used the plural form of the word."

"This has nothing to do with *my* ego," she said. "You're the one who's jealous."

"I know you like to think it's jealousy. But the fact of the matter is that this is about priorities—what really matters in this relationship and what doesn't. When it comes right down to it, your career is all you really care about."

"What about you and your career, Michael?" she countered, growing angrier by the minute. She turned to look as the wind blew the rain hard against the window. "Are you saying that if you got a call from New York with an offer to play the lead in a new Neil Simon play, you wouldn't be on the next plane out of town?"

"We came to Seattle together after discussing it at length," he reminded, sounding terribly reasonable. "This theater might have been my brainchild, but it was our joint endeavor. We were in it together, Dina, and I've considered you a partner from the beginning."

"So now you're trying to lay a guilt trip on me," she accused.

"No, I'm just stating the facts."

"What are you really saying? That you want me to tell Kit I'm not interested in the part because I don't want to hurt your feelings?"

Michael got up and went over to the chair where he'd tossed his clothes. He slipped on his shorts and started dressing.

"Michael," she said, her hands on her hips, "talk to me. I want to know what you expect."

He turned to face her as he buttoned his shirt. "This isn't about a part in Hollywood. It isn't even about our theater. It's about us, Dina. Us."

"Yes, I know it is. And I want to know what you're trying to tell me."

"In theory we're getting married next Saturday," he said nonchalantly. "I canceled all my other plans so I could be there. I was under the impression you had, too. But now it seems another offer has come along." He sat on the chair and began putting on his socks and shoes.

"I have not said I wasn't marrying you on Saturday. I haven't even said I was going down to L.A. for the screen test. All I'm trying to do is discuss it with you. Unfortunately you prefer to make a federal case out of it, get sarcastic and go off in a huff."

He stopped tying his shoes and looked up at her. "I'm not going off in a huff, Geraldine. I'm getting dressed because I don't enjoy arguing with no clothes on. Somehow it's demeaning. But that's not the point, either. I've had a realization about you. It seems you aren't quite as committed to this marriage as I thought. Maybe it's something we need to take another look at."

"My God," she said, slapping her head in exasperation. "You're determined to make this a battle to the death. You're making me choose, aren't you, Michael? You or Hollywood. You won't look at it any other way. There's no give-and-take, no willingness to compromise."

"Some people may be willing to 'sort of' get married, Dina, but I'm not one of them. For me, marriage is like pregnancy—you either are, or you aren't. There's no in-between."

"You're saying if I flew down to L.A. in the morning and was back here the day after...that's not good enough."

He stood, putting his hands on his hips, like her. "It's not whether you go to Los Angeles or not, Dina. It's whether our wedding has to compete for a spot on your calendar."

"All right, since you're giving me an ultimatum, we'll do it your way, Michael. But first, answer the question I asked earlier. What if the director of a new Neil Simon play called. What would *you* do?"

"I'd tell him I'm getting married Saturday."

"I told Kit that."

"And I'd tell him I'm committed to you and to my new theater company."

"You're saying you'd turn him down flat."

"I'm not saying I would never take a special part—that I wouldn't leave to do something really terrific at some point. But if it substantially interfered with what was happening in our personal lives, I wouldn't do it."

"You sound very noble, Michael," she said. "I suppose you're sincere, but the sad fact is I got the call tonight and you didn't, so it's what *I* decide that really matters."

"I do believe you're right about that, Geraldine," he said.

They stared at each other. Neither spoke. Dina saw an obstinacy in him she hadn't seen before. She'd known him long enough to realize he could be stubborn, but this was the first time it had surfaced over something terribly important to both of them. This wasn't a little argument over who was going to have their way. Their lives, their careers, their marriage, were all on the line and she wasn't liking what she was seeing or hearing at all.

"Maybe I've been wrong about us," she said. "I would have liked to think you'd have been happy for me, that you would have encouraged me, that our marriage would have allowed room for our individual endeavors. But I see I'm wrong. There's no room in this marriage for Hollywood—at least, as you see it—and I suppose I have to respect that."

"You have to be true to yourself, Dina, as much as I do."

She drew herself up. "We're talking about ending this, aren't we? Five days before we were to marry, and we're talking about saying goodbye."

"I discovered something about you tonight and you discovered something about me," he said, staring at her with glistening eyes. "Maybe we should consider ourselves fortunate."

"It would be too logical to sleep on this and discuss it in the morning, wouldn't it?" she said.

"I don't see that it matters whether you go to Hollywood for the screen test or whether you get the part or not," he replied. "The issue is much more fundamental than that."

"For once, we agree."

There was an awkward moment, then he said, "We'd better let our families know as soon as possible. You're going to be busy the next couple of days, so I'll notify the minister and the caterer and all that."

His words cut through her like a knife. He spoke them with such coldness. Dina couldn't believe what she'd heard. He was actually taking it to the mat. She felt a profound sadness, heartbreak, a sense of loss.

Dina peered into Michael's eyes, knowing that she loved him, even if she wasn't feeling very charitable toward him right then. She knew and he knew there was a fundamental problem; and yet, the obvious wasn't easy to acknowledge.

"This is no small thing we're doing," she said, her eyes brimming with tears.

"Timing is everything in life," he said. "Maybe we should consider ourselves lucky."

Dina bit her lip. "I've never had to do anything like this before. You've already got a star in the sidewalk with my name on it, and I haven't even had a screen test."

He smiled sadly. "Maybe I know something about you that you don't, Geraldine Winterhalter. Maybe that's why I said the things I did tonight."

Tears ran down her cheeks and Dina wiped them away with the backs of her hands. She didn't want to cry, but there was no stopping it. She felt wretched.

"There is one thing I'd like to ask of you," he said.

"What?" she questioned, sniffling.

"I'd appreciate it if you'd let me know how the test turns out."

She nodded. "I will."

"I've got to be honest, though. I don't want to be the booby prize."

"I understand. If I don't get the part, I won't come back."

"I didn't say that," he said. "You're welcome on my stage anytime."

"No," she said, wiping her eyes. "That would never work. Not considering the way it's been between us."

Michael nodded sadly. Then he slipped on his jacket and got his umbrella from the corner. He stood there in the flickering candlelight, staring at her. Tears continued to course down her cheeks.

"Seattle's great," he said, "though I could do with a little less rain." He went to the door, pausing with his hand on the knob. "I can let myself out. You'd better call Kit."

He left and Dina fell onto the bed, sobbing.

FROM THE WINDOW in the front room of Kit Mosley's one-bedroom apartment in the hills above West Hollywood, Dina could see a tiny wedge of the nighttime skyline. By day she'd hardly been aware of the view. Both days she'd been in town, the city had been sweltering in smog, even though it was only May.

Only May. How odd. For the past four months May 12th was to be the biggest day of her life. And now it was nothing more than the day after tomorrow. Just another Saturday. The last weekend before her movie career was to begin.

And yet, she'd barely given her big break a passing thought. She'd gotten excited and hugged Kit when they'd gotten the call from Sid Berman—Kit's agent who was also Dina's agent now—with word that Barry and Sharon Witt, the producer, wanted her for the part. They'd danced a jig in the tiny living room and they'd opened a bottle of champagne and gulped it down. But after Kit left, Dina had spent the rest of the day thinking about Michael back in Seattle.

She turned from the window and went to the phone again. She'd already called at least five times with no luck, though she hadn't left any messages on his machine. She'd decided she had to tell him the news personally and could hardly expect him to call back, but she was beginning to think that might be the only way she'd ever get to talk to him.

Dina dialed Michael's number. The phone rang in his apartment over a thousand miles up the coast. After the fourth ring the machine answered. She listened to his taped voice and the beep, then said, "Michael, it's Dina. Please call me at Kit's." She repeated the number even though he had it. Then she hung up.

She sat on Kit's Victorian sofa to think. The entire place was decorated with items from used-furniture and antique stores. It was artsy-funky, a reflection of Kit's days as a struggling young actress.

Kit now spent nearly all her time at Barry Stewart's condo in Santa Monica and said that unless and until she and Barry married, she'd keep the apartment as a refuge of last resort and a motel for out-of-town guests. Except for that afternoon when Kit had come by in anticipation of Sid Berman's call, Dina had been alone in the apartment practically the whole time she'd been in L.A. Kit had told her she could stay until her furniture arrived from Seattle, and she found a place of her own.

Things in L.A. were moving ahead with machinelike efficiency. The afternoon she arrived she'd spent an hour at the studio. Barry had seemed pleased with her test. He'd said he wanted to study the footage and talk to Sharon. The decision would come by the next afternoon at the latest, he'd told her.

And it had. Sid had leaned hard on Sharon, knowing Barry's desperation, and he'd gotten Dina good money, considering it was her first film. Six weeks of work on *Sitting Pretty* would pay her more than she'd made in three years in New York and Seattle. Dina knew this could be her big break, and yet she felt strangely empty. Sorry in a way. Guilty.

The night Michael had walked out on her had been like a nightmare, and so had been the next day. She'd stayed by the phone all morning before deciding the crisis was as much or more her doing than his. If she loved the guy—and she did—she could at least reach out to him. So that next afternoon she'd called him.

The first words out of her mouth had been, "Michael, I do love you."

He was silent for a moment, then he'd said. "I believe you, Dina. And I love you."

She'd waited, expecting, hoping, for a word of conciliation. But he'd disappointed her.

"Somehow," he said, "that doesn't seem to matter a whole lot, does it?"

"You really want it to end?" she'd asked with a trembling voice.

"No, I don't want it to. But if we try to ignore what happened, we'd be kidding ourselves."

"Michael, how can we be on the verge of marrying one day and saying goodbye the next? Were we crazy then, or are we crazy now?"

He didn't say anything.

"Tell me, Michael. Which of us is crazy now?"

"Neither of us is," he replied after a minute. "One actress in a thousand gets the opportunity you've got. If I'm really honest, I don't blame you a bit. But I don't want to marry your Hollywood career. Call it selfish, but it's the way I truly feel. And saying so is more fair to you in the long run."

So she'd gotten on a plane to Los Angeles, her heart filled with pain, guilt and resentment. She wasn't convinced Michael had to do what he'd done, but he had. And maybe he was right. She wouldn't have wanted a divorce a year down the line. So maybe Kit's call, coming when it did, was the best thing that could have happened.

Kit's telephone rang, making Dina jump. She went over and grabbed the receiver.

"Is you a star, or is you not?" It was Michael. Her heart leapt at the sound of his voice.

"I got the part," she said softly.

"That's terrific! Really terrific," he said enthusiastically.

He sounded like he meant it. Michael was an actor, but she also knew him. She knew how to separate what was false in him from what was genuine.

Dina pictured his pale, pale blue eyes and that grin of his that was so distinctive. Michael Cross was not the ruggedly handsome type, nor did he have a pretty-boy face. His looks fell somewhere in between. He was appealing, yet he had character—the perfect combination for an actor. Michael could project so many different personas. Above all, he was a leading man. The truth was that he belonged in films—as much as or more than she did.

"Shooting starts Monday," she told him. "I considered coming back to get my things, but decided to have everything sent down here instead."

He hesitated. "Do you want me to arrange it?" he asked, his voice low.

"No. Thank you for offering but I already called Mary. She's lusted after my place for months and agreed to sublet it. I made packing my stuff and sending it off part of the deal. You'll want your things, too, Michael. Do you mind working out getting them with her?"

"That's no problem."

Dina wasn't quite sure what to say next. A big part of her wanted to throw caution aside and blurt out, "Oh, the hell with this. I'm coming home. We're getting married on Saturday and that's that!" But she suspected that even if she did say it, Michael wouldn't buy it. Even though it was in anger, he'd said something very insightful that rainy night when he'd walked out. They'd discovered something about each other, and also, something about themselves.

"There's one thing I want you to know, Michael," she finally said. "I'm coming away from this with a very deep scar. We had more than just a relationship. I'll never be the same."

"Is that a compliment or a complaint?"

He was trying to sound glib, but Dina heard the hurt in his voice. Nobody would have picked it up onstage, but she heard it distinctly. "It's both," she said. "I love you, but I also think you're a bastard."

"Well, the feeling is entirely mutual, I assure you."

Dina laughed and so did he. She laughed hard and long. She laughed until she began to cry. Michael listened, comforting with his presence.

She sniffled, wiping her nose. "Well, there's no point in dragging this out. Have a good life, Michael," she said.

"You have a good life, too, Geraldine Winterhalter. When I see your name in lights I'll be proud of you. I want you to know that. And I'll never miss a single one of your movies."

She began sobbing silently, then. She couldn't talk. All she managed was a breathy, anguished, "Goodbye."

1

"NO, DAMN IT!" Dina said, pacing. "Absolutely not!"

Sid Berman sat behind his enormous glass desk, the view of Beverly Hills and Westwood from twenty-three floors up spreading out behind him. His fingers were steepled under his chin as he stared at her. With a corner office and that view, Sid undoubtedly felt like God, and Dina knew he was Hollywood's hottest agent right now, but she didn't care about things like that. Other people could fall at his feet and kiss his toes. She wasn't going to prostitute herself. She simply wasn't!

"Taking a practical look at things is not easy for an artist, I know, Dina," he said, "but—"

"Oh, Sid, for God's sake don't patronize me. I'm fully capable of looking at the business side of the issue. Having strong opinions does not make me a temperamental starlet, some bimbo you have to flatter into submission."

"Okay, let me cut through the crap and lay it on the line," he said. "Your career, your film career, while not exactly in the toilet, is presently hovering on the rim and ready to topple in. If that's not graphic enough, let me put it this way. In this town you're only as good as your last film. Since you won your Oscar for best supporting actress in *Sitting Pretty*, you've had two duds in a row."

"The critics liked my performance in *Mirabella*."

"Yes, but they hated the film," Sid said, running his fingers back through his permed gray hair. "And it wasn't too popular at the box office, either." He was fifty, slender, and had a penchant for neatly tailored Italian suits. "Look, Dina, you've been true to your artistic instincts, and I respect that. But let's be honest. Bottom line, end of the day, art's got nothing to do with anything that really counts in this town."

"Yes," she said. "You're saying I should be doing films like *Revenge of the Ghouls*." She looked over at him. "'A sure commercial hit.' Wasn't that the way you phrased it when you sold me on that part?"

Sid nodded sadly, conceding the point. "That was my fault, Dina. I admit it. I got suckered. I never should have put you in that picture. But it was your second film and before we knew you were getting the Oscar. I wanted you in a lead."

"There's no point in haggling over spilled milk," she said. "I followed your mistake with a doozy of my own."

"So that brings us back to the question at hand," he said. "Do we do the Michael Cross picture, or don't we?"

"I've already given you my answer," she said. "Absolutely not."

"Yeah, I know those were your words, doll, but I've got to hear your reasoned, unemotional explanation. Do you really want me to tell Cross to stick it?"

"You obviously don't believe I'm capable of saying no."

"Before I accept it, I gotta understand it," he said.

Dina sighed, folding her arms over her breast. She hadn't told Sid, or anyone else for that matter, that she'd come within days of marrying Michael Cross five years earlier. And as far as she knew, Michael had never mentioned it in interviews, or let it get into the gossip columns. Kit Mosley was her only friend in the business who was aware of the broken engagement, and Kit had been very discreet.

It all seemed so long ago and far away. She hadn't even *seen* Michael since that last, awful night in Seattle. She'd scarcely spent any time in L.A., having gone straight to London after *Revenge of the Ghouls*, and before Michael came to Hollywood.

She had been in London when Michael's first big blockbuster hit the screen. Who would have believed an obscure actor somebody had seen doing repertory in Seattle would become Hollywood's next big action hero? So for the past few years, while she'd been licking her wounds on the other side of the Atlantic, Michael was becoming the most-mentioned name on every fifteen-year-old boy's lips—to the tune of one-hundred-and-fifty million dollars a pop.

Dina was glad for his success, of course, because she'd always wished him well. But she was a little sad, too, because she honestly believed Michael's talents were bigger than the work he was doing. Still, when you came right down to it, she needed his sympathy a hell of a lot more than he needed hers. She'd had a shot and blown it, though perhaps not irrevocably. Everybody agreed that one big smash hit and she'd be right back in the running.

"So what's the problem?" Sid asked. "Is it Cross, or his picture?"

"Both."

"That isn't very helpful, if you don't mind me saying so."

"Does it matter, Sid?" she argued. "I don't want to do the movie. Isn't that enough?"

He gave her an inquiring look and tapped his chin with his finger. "You know, Cross asked for you personally. He called me up and wanted to know if you'd be available to do the female lead in his picture. It's called *Cold Hearts*, by the way."

"Michael personally asked for me?"

"Yes. He's also producer, you know. He stands to make fifty million dollars on the film if it's as successful as the last two. And he made us a very generous offer, Dina. Double what he has to pay for the role."

"People tend to throw money around when they have it."

"I don't think that's it." Sid got up from behind his desk, stretching as he walked around it. "I know I'm only your agent, but the more I know about the parties involved in a negotiation, the better chance I have of handling it successfully. Is there something between you and Michael Cross I should know about?"

"I've known him since I broke into theater in New York seven or eight years ago."

"You're old pals, then."

"In a manner of speaking."

Sid stood looking at her, his hands on his hips. "So what's the problem? You'd rather do another artsy-fartsy picture with Mason Fellows than get your face in every newspaper and on half the screens in America?"

"Mason wants to do a film of Lillian Phelps's novel *Green September*. He holds the option and he's already written the screenplay, Sid. That's why he came with me to L.A.—to round up financing for the project, while I figure out what I'm going to do."

He contemplated her again. "Forgive me if this question is indiscreet, but is it my imagination, or are you and Fellows joined at the hip?"

Dina drew an impatient breath. "We've considered marriage. Mason has asked me to marry him."

"And?"

"Let's just say it's still under discussion." She could see he didn't like the sidestepping. "I'll probably accept, if you must know. But Mason will be the first to hear my decision. Not my agent."

"I had no idea it was that serious," he said, his voice more solemn than usual. "Congratulations." He didn't sound sincere.

"Thanks, but hold the congratulations for the time being."

"It's your life, doll."

"I know you don't think a lot of Mason," she said. "He's not a Hollywood type. He plays the game less well than I do, even. But he's terribly talented, even if he doesn't have the most commercial instincts."

Sid Berman smiled slightly, but kept his mouth shut. Dina knew full well that Sid had long blamed Mason for the tailspin her career had been in. Mason was the one who'd talked her into doing *Othello* on the stage in London, and though she'd done more than just a credible job, the critics had had a field day with her—more because she was the girl from *Revenge of the Ghouls* than for anything she did on the boards.

Since *Othello* she'd done some good work for the BBC and had gotten great reviews playing Maggie in a London revival of *Cat on a Hot Tin Roof*—but only a few critics and tourists west of the Atlantic were even aware of that.

Mirabella was Mason's first feature-length film that had been distributed in America. He'd written the original screenplay and directed it. It had been a colossal flop at the box office, although the few accolades that had been passed out were for Dina's performance. Still, she'd suffered from having been associated with the project. The film had done better in Britain, but as Sid correctly pointed out, she was unlikely to make it big as an actress in England, either in film or on the stage. If she was going to have a major career, it would have to be in Hollywood or New York. She knew all too well she was at a crossroads.

Dina went to one of Sid's two big gray leather sofas and sat down, crossing her legs. It was October and still quite warm in southern California. She was wearing a little sleeveless Armani dress that showed a lot of leg. Sid, who only recently had divorced his second wife to marry a client, was not above noticing a woman's legs. But to his credit, he was never obvious.

"I think it's time for straight talk," she said. "After all, I pay you for your advice, Sid."

He seemed to brighten at the prospect and came to sit in the other sofa, across from her. "I can be as straight with you as you could possibly hope, Dina. You know that."

"Okay," she said in her no-nonsense tone. "Assuming Mason gets the money to do *Green September*, is playing the lead a good or a bad move, career-wise?"

"My guess is you won't have to worry about him getting the money. Not after *Mirabella*. Even assuming he pulls it off somehow, I'd have to see the script and know who the male lead is before I could say for sure. My off-the-top-of-the-head guess is that your odds of profiting from it are one in five, maybe one in three."

"What if I do Michael's film first?"

He thought for a moment. "If you do really well in *Cold Hearts*, you might be able to carry *Green September*, assuming all the other pieces are there."

"What if Michael produces *Green September*, Sid? Is it more likely to go, then?"

"Cross doing Fellows's film? Why would he do something completely out of his genre?"

"Michael wasn't always a shoot-'em-up action-movie hero, Sid. He's actually a fine actor. Honestly, I think it's sad that he sold his soul to the devil to do those films he's done. He's much better than that."

"Yeah, well, save your pity for yourself, doll. Cross doesn't need it. But tell me, were you asking a serious question, or were you running off at the mouth?"

"It was a serious question. Will you ask Michael if he'd consider doing *Green September*?"

"I could, but seeing that you're old pals, Dina, why don't you ask him yourself? Cross told me he'd like to meet with you, if I could get you interested enough to talk about the picture."

"He wanted to meet with me?"

"Sure. For breakfast, lunch. Whatever."

Dina stopped to think. She wondered why Michael was so eager to see her. She knew he hadn't married, but like any man with a little clout in Hollywood, he wouldn't have lacked for companionship, though she had no idea of the specifics because there'd been almost no communication between them. After she'd won her Oscar, he'd sent her a dozen roses and a card of congratulations. She'd written a thank-you note and that had been it.

She'd gone to see his first film when it opened in London, and she'd cried—and not for any reason having to do with the story. It had just seemed so amazing to see the man she'd once loved up there on the screen, bigger than life. She hadn't seen his last two films. In the meantime she'd fallen for Mason. Her future was with him. Michael Cross was a ghost from the past—or at least had been until now.

Dina was torn. She'd told Sid, "No, absolutely not." Yet here she was, thinking about it, trying to figure out how—by prostituting herself to Michael Cross and his hundred-million-dollar movie—she might further her career and help Mason at the same time.

"What'll it be, Dina?" Sid asked. "Will you dance with the gentleman, or won't you?"

She thought of the way Michael used to make love with her—a vision she hadn't conjured up in a very long time—and she shivered. "Dance with him?" she echoed.

"He didn't say anything about stayin' the night, doll. I can only assume his intentions are honorable. Actually, what he said was, 'See if she'll have breakfast or lunch with me.'"

Dina folded her hands nervously. "Better make it lunch," she decided, leaning back with a sigh.

God knew, there had been a time when she'd regularly had breakfast with Michael Cross. More than once, he'd laid her on the breakfast table. Michael could be deadly. No, she thought, breakfast wouldn't be good. Lunch would be better.

When she stopped to think about it, though, she realized Michael could be pretty awesome at just about any time of day. And even if he played it straight and kept to business, seeing him would not be easy. Not easy at all.

EARLY THE NEXT MORNING Mason Fellows swept into the sitting room of their suite at the Bel Air Hotel. "God, how I hate this town. Everyone is so bloody mercenary."

Dina looked over at him and smiled. Mason was tall and lanky and dressed with the carelessness so typical of Brits. She tended to attribute it to his eccentricity rather than simply being disheveled, although that was equally descriptive of the way he looked.

"It's no different in London," Dina replied evenly. "The style's different, that's all." She was still in her nightgown, sitting in an armchair by the open sliding-glass doors, having a tall glass of fresh-squeezed orange juice while she waited for Mason to emerge from his room.

Mason, with a tag of tissue on his chin where he'd nicked himself shaving, leaned over and kissed her cheek. "One can be mercenary with or without civility, love," he said. "Hollywood folk wouldn't recognize good manners if they bit them on the ass."

"Don't get yourself in a mood," she warned. "It won't help your cause with that studio executive you're meeting. Just pour on that English charm of yours during breakfast. Civil or not, this town is a sucker for a British accent."

"Oh, they love me well enough. But will they give me their bloody money to make my film? That, after all, is the important question."

Dina took his hand. "Did you sleep well, Mason? You look a bit tired."

In all the months they'd been together, they'd never spent an entire night in the same bed. Mason couldn't sleep unless he had a bed to himself, in his own room. "Too many years boarding in public schools," he'd explained. "Having discovered the joys of nocturnal solitude, I can never go back."

Mason ran his fingers back through his thick sandy hair. "Scarcely slept a wink. Too bleeding nervous," he said with a laugh.

"It'll work out somehow, darling," she told him. "Don't worry."

He brushed her cheek with his knuckles and smiled, his long, angular face looking handsome in a peculiarly English way. "And what have you planned for today?" he asked.

"I'm having lunch with Michael Cross."

"Cross? Whatever for?"

"Sid believes there's a chance I could snag the lead in Michael's next film, *Cold Hearts*. He wants me to talk to him."

"I should think an action thriller would be the last thing you'd take on, love. I can't see you shooting flaming arrows or hurling hand grenades whilst cavorting in a bikini."

Dina had never told him about her relationship with Michael—not so much out of a desire to conceal anything as because of the understanding they had. Mason didn't ask about her past and she didn't inquire about his. She wasn't sure what to attribute it to, except that Mason was very pragmatic and not in the least jealous. In fact, he could be dispassionate down to his toenails.

"I think there may be more substance to the role in this one," she said, "and that's part of the reason I'm to meet with Michael. Sid wanted me to get it directly from the horse's mouth."

Dina knew she was being a trifle dishonest, but she saw no point in making an issue of something Mason couldn't care less about. Besides, he had larger concerns.

"I should think it will be an interesting lunch," Mason said. "The man has a presence, doesn't he? I wouldn't mind meeting Cross myself, if ever I have the chance."

"You were invited to lunch, Mason, but I declined for you. I hope you don't mind. Frankly, I assumed you'd prefer to concentrate your energies on *Green September*."

"Quite right. I shouldn't want to let you down, however, if you'd prefer that I come along."

"I wouldn't trouble you. To tell you the truth, I don't expect anything to come of it. And you have much more important things to do."

"You're a darling to understand. But do tell Cross I regret having to forgo the pleasure of his company and that I hope to meet him one day."

"I will, Mason."

"If he offers you something, mind you don't commit yourself to anything that would interfere with *Green*

September," he added. "You and you alone are my leading lady. The role of Clarice was made for you. Making sure you play her was the principal reason I've taken on the project."

Dina knew that was only half the story, though she suspected he needed to believe that was true. Mason felt guilty about what had happened with *Mirabella* and he was anxious to direct her in a successful venture.

"And your picture is the most important thing in my life, too, darling," she said, patting his cheek. That, at least, was true. If push came to shove she'd make Mason—or at least, their personal relationship—her top priority. She'd learned the hard way that putting her career first caused more problems than it solved.

"You're a love." Mason checked his watch. "I must be off. I hope your discussions with Mr. Cross are fruitful."

"I'm not optimistic," she replied. It was true. She wasn't.

He grabbed his worn briefcase and headed for the door.

"Oh, darling," she called after him. "Don't forget to take off that bit of tissue on your chin before your appointment."

He pulled the tissue from his face, blew her a kiss, and went out the door. Dina took another long swig of juice, then, without intending it, had another recollection of her breakfasts with Michael. Knowing that was a dangerous course, she gulped down the rest of her drink and went off to have her bath.

MICHAEL CROSS'S HOUSE sat on a hilltop in Brentwood with a view extending as far as the haze and smog would

allow. Driving up the street in a taxi, having seen all of
the multimillion-dollar homes lining the way, Dina had
anticipated that his place would be sumptuous. But it
wasn't until they pulled through the gate that she fully
appreciated how a man making millions of dollars a year
lived.

The house was low, modern, and rambled over the
crest of the hill as though God had planned it that way.
The landscaping was surprisingly lush, considering how
new the house was. Perhaps Michael had brought in fully
grown trees and shrubs. William Randolph Hearst had
at San Simeon. Why not the preeminent superhero of
modern films?

She went up the flagstone steps, suddenly feeling
nervous. It had been five years since she'd seen Michael
and her fear brought on a crisis of confidence—good old-
fashioned stage fright. Reaching for the doorbell, her
hand trembled. Right then, she knew that she'd almost
certainly made a mistake in coming. But it was too late
now.

Michael answered the door. He was in a pair of faded
jeans and a pink polo shirt and loafers without socks.
She'd forgotten the magic of those pale, pale blue eyes of
his, even though the cinematographers had stamped
them on every one of his films like a logo. Her heart
tripped as they stared at each other, and Michael's expression quickly turned into a smile of delight.

He looked beyond her at the taxi disappearing down
the drive. "Where's Mason?"

"He had a meeting with one of the studios this morning and couldn't make it back in time."

He gestured for her to enter. "Will he be joining us later?"

She walked past him, inhaling a cologne she didn't recognize. It was crisp and fresh, as unfamiliar as Michael's newfound status. She felt the scent all the way down in her gut. As he closed the door, she turned on the granite tiles in the entry to face him. "I don't think so. Mason's awfully busy, but he did want to come. Truly. He's a fan of yours, Michael. And so am I, for that matter."

He smiled, stepped over and took both her arms, holding her as he looked her over. "Bull. My fans—apart from the guys who finance my films—are within spitting distance of puberty." He grinned. "You look damn good, Dina."

"So do you, Michael."

Gazing into his eyes, she remembered those sexy breakfasts and even sexier candlelit nights. She recalled the feel of his skin, and the taste of his mouth when he kissed her.

She turned away to take in her surroundings. Michael let go of her arms and they walked slowly back through the house. It was Mediterranean in style but the furnishings were eclectic—an antique table, a modern mirror, antique silver chandelier, a Cubist painting that might have been a Picasso.

"I won't show you the house," he said teasingly. "It would take till dinnertime."

"Your success is no secret," she replied. Glancing at him, she smiled. "I'm very happy for you, Michael. You deserve it."

He scoffed. "You think I'm a whore. But that's okay—I do, too."

They laughed as he led her back to a solarium filled with large plants, comfortable wicker furniture, orchids, ferns, a waterfall and a pool with lily pads and eight-inch carp. The glass wall opposite the sofa where they sat afforded a view of the Pacific—a strip of blue in the far distance.

She glanced at Michael. She'd expected that once they began talking, her nervousness would abate some, but instead it was getting worse. She drew a breath to calm herself.

"How about a margarita before we eat?" he asked.

"I usually don't drink this early."

"You're back in California, Dina. There won't be tea at four, but you can have a margarita or a mimosa anytime you wish." He winked. "Besides, it'll settle our nerves to have a drink."

"You think they need settling?"

"Mine do. It's been over five years, and the last time I saw you we were engaged. Remember?"

"How could I forget?"

"Had it not been for *Sitting Pretty*, we might be sitting pretty together now, as man and wife. Our son would be about two or so."

"Our son?"

"Yeah, you'd said you didn't want to wait more than a couple of years to have kids. Better, you said, they be in college before I have my mid-life crisis."

"I said that?"

"Yeah. One February night in Seattle. It was raining, of course. I was pouring hot toddies down you, declaring that I had an overwhelming urge to get you pregnant."

She colored. "Oh," she said, nodding. "That is starting to sound familiar. I'd forgotten all about it."

"I haven't. I think of it often, actually."

Their eyes met. Dina fought him till she finally had to look away. "This isn't the wisest line of conversation," she said. "I think I will have that margarita, if you don't mind."

He got up and went to the intercom by the door, and ordered drinks. He returned to the sofa. "So, Mason couldn't make it. Do I get to meet him another time?"

"Perhaps. Depending on how things work out."

"How serious is it? Your relationship, I mean."

"We're very close," she said.

"What, exactly, does that mean?"

"We're considering marrying. We've had serious discussions about it."

"What's holding you up? Waiting for the queen's blessing, or an opening in your schedule?"

She ignored the jab, choosing to respond obliquely. "Mason and I try to be supportive of one another. We do everything we can to avoid putting pressure on the relationship." She looked into Michael's eyes to see how he was taking her counterpunch. He seemed unfazed.

"What are you saying, Dina? That Mason hasn't given you an ultimatum yet?"

Ultimatums. That was what had doomed their relationship—Michael's demands. "Mason's not the type who issues ultimatums," she answered evenly.

"God knows, that's the type you deserve," he said, actually sounding sincere. "But don't take anything for granted. Believe me. I know from personal experience that things can backfire on you when you least expect it. I learned that lesson the hard way."

"Yes," she said, controlling her emotions. "I learned the same lesson."

As they exchanged looks, the housekeeper, a stout gray-haired woman in her fifties, arrived with a pitcher of margaritas. Michael poured and handed Dina her glass. "Well," he said, toasting her, "to avoiding repeating mistakes."

"Cheers." She took a sip to cover the blush spreading across her face.

"I liked *Mirabella*, by the way," he said. "And not just your performance, which was superb. Mason did a creditable job directing. But the screenplay needed work."

"Mason wrote it, Michael."

"Oh. Well, he should have called in a script doctor."

"Mason is very proud."

"That's not a positive attribute in this business," he said.

"Yes," Dina said, taking another sip of her margarita. "I know."

"I'm hardly one to criticize serious filmmakers," he said humbly. "But like everyone, I've got my opinions."

He looked at her over the rim of his glass and Dina felt her insides quiver. She hadn't expected him to have this effect on her. She'd been so sure she'd gotten beyond this sort of thing—beyond being affected by Michael's animal magnetism.

She felt his eyes on her, but she didn't meet his gaze. She couldn't. Not until she'd calmed down.

"I watched *Sitting Pretty* so many times I finally wore the cassette out," he said. "I had to buy another copy."

She chuckled nervously. "That was the only role I didn't make a mistake on."

"You were beautiful. Magnificent. Your Oscar was well deserved."

"Thank you, Michael," she said, engaging his eyes. "But the past isn't relevant. We've all moved on, haven't we?"

"The question is if it's been for the better."

She got the message, but chose not to call him on it. "You've certainly done well. I've enjoyed your work, even if I am beyond spitting range of puberty, as you put it."

"It's a living."

"You're much too modest," she said.

He drained his glass and poured them both more. "I want a serious actress for my next film—someone whose chemistry is perfect with mine," he said. "Since I'm producing, I've got complete control, and there's only one woman for the role. You."

"I'm flattered," she said. "Truly. But I must be honest. I seriously doubt that it's wise for us to be together."

He studied her. "Are we talking professionally or personally?"

"Both."

He sipped his drink. "Which do you want to discuss first?"

She held her glass by the stem, turning it unconsciously. "I've a question that involves both, I suppose."

"Shoot."

"Why do you want me in your picture, Michael? I mean, why do you *really* want me in it?"

"By that I take it you don't accept my reasoning."

"I'm not special. There are a dozen other actresses who could easily do the role. So that can't be it."

"Have you read the script?" he asked.

"No, but—"

"But how could it be any different from the female lead in my other films?" he said, finishing the question for her.

"I've only seen your first, Michael."

He laughed, his white teeth gleaming. "Some fan you are, Geraldine Winterhalter!"

Dina turned crimson.

"That's all right. I never see them after looking at the final cut, either," he said. "But to return to the point, the chemistry between the leads will make or break the film. There has to be fire."

She gulped her margarita. "Which brings us to the other point."

"Whether this is a wise thing to do, personally?" he suggested.

"Our past can't be ignored."

He stroked his chin. "What are you afraid of?"

"I'm not afraid."

"Then what is your concern?"

She gathered her courage. "I have to know that you regard this as strictly professional."

He chuckled. "You're saying you don't want me to enjoy the love scenes."

"I don't care what you do on the set," she retorted. "But I would want an understanding as to what happens *off* the set."

His expression turned serious. "You mean you don't want me to seduce you."

She gave him a look. "I don't want you to even try."

"Do you want it in your contract, or will you take my word?"

"Michael, aren't you being a little glib? I'm not here on a date. I was invited to talk business."

He put down his margarita. "Yes, Dina, you were."

She continued fingering her glass. "I like to feel good about a project before I sign on. And I must confess, I don't feel good about doing a picture with you."

"Sid Berman said you had some conditions before you'd take the part. If hashing them out is why you're here, maybe we should discuss them first."

Dina was embarrassed to think that she'd actually laid down "conditions" for working with him. It made her feel cheap, like she was a sharp dealer. She drained her glass. But when she took a deep breath, she knew it had been a big mistake to drink so much on an empty stomach. She could feel the effects already. Even so, she didn't object when Michael refilled her glass. She picked it up immediately and engaged his eyes, drawing on all the fortitude she had in her.

"All right, let's discuss my conditions for doing your film," she said.

"You want me to produce Mason's current project. Lillian Phelps's novel. Right?"

"Yes. I'd like you to at least take a look at it."

He thought for a moment. "Are you making it a condition, or aren't you?"

"Well, I don't want to blackmail you."

"Sweetheart, blackmail is probably the only way you can get me to do a film like that. Eighteenth-century love stories aren't big these days."

Dina's anger flared. "How can you say that, Michael? You haven't seen the script."

"Mason wrote it, didn't he?"

"Yes."

"I've seen *Mirabella*."

She fumed, glaring. "Haven't you ever had a failure?"

"So far, my mistakes have carried price tags under a million dollars," he said. "Knock on wood. But let's not quibble. Have Mason send me a copy of the script, and I'll look it over."

Dina hung her head. "I haven't told him about this yet."

He contemplated her, then broke into a grin. "A chicken-and-egg problem, huh?" he prompted, chuckling.

She nodded.

"I would say this negotiation has reached the reading stage. You've got to read the screenplay to *Cold Hearts* and I've got to read . . . what is it called?"

"*Green September*."

"Right. Then, after we've evaluated each of them, we can put our heads together and see where we are."

"Sounds reasonable," she said.

Michael's eyes gleamed as he appraised her. His expression told her he wasn't thinking about business. He was looking at the woman he hadn't married, the woman who could have given him a child.

Dina couldn't help regarding him in much the same way. Michael Cross, after all, was the man her mother had wanted for a son-in-law. For months after the wedding was called off, Bernice Winterhalter had asked after him, hoping Dina would have news. She'd finally given up, but Bernice had made no bones about the breakup having been a mistake.

"Will we be eating soon, Michael?" Dina asked. "I've got to be getting back to the hotel at a reasonable hour. Mason will be waiting."

"Sure. Let's finish off the pitcher," he said, pouring, "and then eat."

Dina took refuge in her margarita. It was a coward's way, she knew, but at the moment, numbing herself with alcohol seemed the best way to deal with things. If she let herself, she could imagine going off to Michael's sumptuous bedroom with him. They would make wild, passionate love. It would be fabulous. And it could happen, if she'd let it.

But afterward she'd hate herself. That wasn't what she really wanted. What she cared about most, what she had to focus on, was Mason.

Yet, when she looked into Michael's eyes, she knew if she were to do a love scene with him, especially one in which they were naked, she'd be lost. She'd be crazy to even consider it.

Seeing the look in his eye, Dina knew why she hadn't allowed herself to see him over the past five years. Being around Michael was the worst sort of temptation a woman could experience. And yet, career-wise, there was so much to be gained if she did his film. The bottom line was, he had her right where he wanted her. And the bastard knew it, too.

2

THE HOUSEKEEPER SERVED lunch in the sunroom. There was grilled red snapper, served with rice and lightly sautéed vegetables, and a bottle of Chardonnay. But after the margaritas, Dina decided to pass on the wine. This was serious business, whether Michael wanted her to treat it that way or not.

He kept her talking by asking about England and her work there. Dina didn't mind the questions—she was grateful for any excuse to bring up Mason. The way she figured it, if she talked about him enough, Michael would eventually understand how important Mason was to her, how she truly had moved beyond the romance and sex of their own past relationship.

Michael listened attentively. In the back of her mind, Dina couldn't help but be pleased that he hadn't let his success go to his head. And yet there was no denying that his achievements in a cutthroat industry had given him a degree of confidence that she hadn't seen in him before. She knew he was probably even more dangerous because of it, but he was being very subtle so as not to make her more wary than she already was.

As the conversation progressed, Dina felt her guard starting to drop. When she noticed that happening, she reminded herself how unwise it would be to fall into old behavior patterns with Michael. The trick would be proving that to him. She'd been talking at length about the joy of working with a man of Mason's talent when there was a lull in the conversation. Dina took a deep breath and watched Michael watching her.

"It's nice to see you haven't changed," he said amiably.

She blinked. "But I *have* changed. That's exactly what I've been telling you."

He shook his head. "No, you haven't. Not really. Not in the ways that matter."

Dina wasn't sure whether to be offended or not. "What's that supposed to mean?"

"It means I'm happy to see you're the person I once knew. I was afraid that time, and being in this business, might have done something to you. It hasn't. You're the Geraldine Winterhalter I once loved and still— Well, let's say, for whom I still have the utmost respect."

"Thank you, Michael. I know you mean that as a compliment. But five long years have passed. I'm older, wiser and more aware of who I really am now. Even if I haven't changed—and I think you're wrong when you say I haven't—I'm in a different place these days. Mason and I are very much in love."

He contemplated her—not exactly in a critical way, but not in a particularly contented way, either. "You seem pretty adamant about him. He pops up in every third paragraph."

"I'm sorry if that disappoints you, Michael. But it's honest."

"Is it really?"

Dina grimaced. She'd never liked being challenged about her feelings, and Michael damn well knew it. In spite of what she'd said about being a different woman, that hadn't changed. "You might as well know that Mason and I are going to marry," she said. "That ought to tell you everything you need to know."

"Well, I'm happy for you even if I do have misgivings."

"Misgivings?"

"What I mean is, I prefer remembering you as you were, Dina."

She blotted her lips with her napkin and sighed. "I was reluctant to come here, but I'm glad now that I did. Whether we end up doing business or not, there was a chapter in my life that never was properly closed and I think I've managed to do that. I feel better."

He gave her an ironic grin. "Well, I'm glad you do."

"I'd like for it to be all right with you, too, Michael. If we do end up working together, it would be so much better."

"You wish to deny me even a wistful glance in your direction, with fond memories of things past?"

She slowly nodded. "I'm afraid so. For both our sakes."

"Wistful feels better," he said.

He wasn't giving up easily, she could see that. "I want you to meet Mason," she said. "That will help you to understand."

His grin broadened. "You have even less understanding of the male psyche than I thought, Dina, my love."

She gave him a tight smile. "You're a big boy, Michael. I'm sure you'll handle it fine."

"I'll do my best."

Dina felt a wave of triumph, but at the same time a twinge of uncertainty. She wasn't absolutely sure she was the one with the upper hand. Michael's words said one thing; his tone of voice, another. But at least she'd made her feelings clear, and that had been one of her main goals.

She looked at her watch. "I hate to eat and run, but I do have to get going."

"We've got things set in motion," he said. "So it was time well spent."

The way he put it, Dina couldn't be sure whether he was referring to business or to them. She wanted to think it was business—that there wouldn't be any problems from here on out. But she knew Michael well enough to know complacency toward him could be dangerous.

"Maybe someone could call me a taxi."

"Not necessary. My driver is waiting to take you home."

"Thank you. I appreciate that." Looking into his eyes, she felt a touch of embarrassment. "If you don't mind, I'll be on my way, then."

"I do mind, but I can hardly keep you here against your will."

Dina opened her mouth to reply, but then decided to let it pass. After all, she wasn't absolutely sure what he meant by it. She got up and so did he. "It was a lovely lunch," she said. "And it was good seeing you again, Michael."

"Yes, we waited much too long."

They slowly walked through the house toward the entry.

"I'm looking forward to reading *Cold Hearts*," she said.

"And I'm eager for a look at *Green September*."

"Don't read it with too critical an eye. Mason is really quite literary. He doesn't like to compromise for the sake of commercial advantage, but he can be persuaded. So keep an open mind."

"You, I take it, are the persuader."

"Mason listens to me," she said.

When they got to the entry, Michael went to a side table and picked up a bound script, handing it to her. It was the screenplay of *Cold Hearts*. She looked down at it.

"I didn't bring *Green September* with me, but I'll have it couriered over this afternoon."

"I'll look forward to seeing it."

Dina fingered the manuscript, already feeling the discomfort of their impending goodbye. Michael still had his effect on her, despite everything. Yet there was one more piece of business to take care of. She agonized for a moment, then plunged ahead.

"Michael, there is one thing. Mason isn't aware that you and I were once engaged. It's not that I've hidden it from him or anything like that. We just don't talk much about the past. That's the way our relationship has developed."

"And you feel knowing about our engagement would be a problem to him?"

"No, it's not that. Mason is not the jealous type. Still, I'm reluctant to bring it up—at least right now. I want him to be able to concentrate on *Green September* to the exclusion of everything else."

"I can be discreet, if that's what you're asking," he said.

"Once we've each read the scripts and made our decisions, I'll have no problem if our engagement comes up. Better the three of us laugh about it over a drink than at the negotiating table. I hope you understand."

"I do. I'll be discreet until you tell me it's okay to talk about it openly."

Dina felt foolish, like a sneak. She hadn't expected that. Asking Michael not to bring up their past had seemed perfectly sensible when she planned it, but now she felt like a coward. Worse, by entering into a conspiracy of silence with him, she was afraid he might start acting as if they were allies. God knows, that was the last thing she needed. But it was too late now.

"It's really no big deal," she said. "I just wanted you to be aware."

He nodded, smiling, looking as if he genuinely understood her situation and sympathized. But she was suspicious. Michael was being a little *too* accommodating.

When he extended his hand, she hesitated before taking it. His grip tightened and he clasped her hand in both of his. Dina suddenly had a very strong sense of him—the Michael Cross who had been her lover, her fiancé. The awareness was intense. And most disturbing. Much more so than she'd expected.

How could it seem as if no time had passed at all? When she looked at him, she saw the man who'd loved her, the one who'd seemed destined to father her children. She quickly reminded herself that was long past. Mason was the man she loved. Mason.

Dina tried hard to conjure up his face, but she couldn't. It was Michael who commanded her attention. Being with him again was like a trip into the past; all the old feelings came surging back to her.

"Thanks again for lunch," she said, when the silence hanging between them became unbearable. "I'll call you after I've read the script."

He paused before responding. "Dina, I don't want to make things hard, but there is something I'd like to say before you go."

The gravity of his tone sent a shiver down her spine. She extricated her hand and looked into his eyes. "Yes?"

"You said earlier that you felt there was a chapter in your life that hadn't been properly closed until today. Well, I feel the same. I've been living with the feeling that things weren't resolved between us. I made a terrible mistake five years ago. I was pigheaded and foolish. My ego got in the way of good judgment. That was wrong, and I want you to know it."

Dina didn't know what to say. "Well, it's behind us now, Michael. Everything has worked out for the best."

"Not for me."

She felt a little bewildered, unsure what he was really trying to say. "I'm sorry," she said after a moment.

He smiled. "I'm not saying that for sympathy. It's my attempt to set the record straight and get my true feelings on record. Letting you get away was the biggest mistake of my life—one I'll have to live with."

"Thanks for saying that. But I'm enough of a fatalist to believe that things happen for a reason."

"We'll see, won't we?"

There was more hope than regret in his voice, and Dina found that unsettling. She reached for the door. "You'll be getting *Green September* this afternoon."

Michael reached out to hold the door closed, taking her arm with his other hand. "Dina, isn't there a tiny part of you that wonders about us?"

She looked him in the eye. "I love Mason. And unless you're willing to accept that, I don't want to see you again. I won't be in your film."

He nodded. "You give me little choice."

"Sorry, Michael. Those are my conditions."

He released the door and stepped back. "I look forward to getting his script."

"We're hopeful you'll like it. I mean, really like it."

"I hope so, too."

Dina escaped into the sunshine. She went to the limousine without looking back. The driver opened the passenger door. She climbed in. Her heart was pounding so hard she could feel her pulse surging in her temples. She sat staring straight ahead, fingering the script on her lap.

A moment later the driver, a young slender Hispanic, was behind the wheel. He started the engine and looped around to head back down the drive. Dina glanced toward the house as they swung past. Michael was still standing at the door, watching. She didn't turn to look at him. She didn't want to see him.

As they approached the gate Dina's eyes were closed, her fists clenched. It had been a mistake to come: Michael wouldn't make it easy for her. She knew now that she would have to fight him every step of the way—if she wanted his help with *Green September*. But in the end she'd prevail, because it was Mason she loved now. And there was nothing Michael could do to change that. Nothing.

DURING THE DRIVE BACK to the hotel Dina began reading the script. He was right about one thing—her character, Alice, was not the usual bimbo that populated action films. She was a lieutenant on the San Francisco police force, and her assignment was to bust a ring of drug smugglers.

When she noticed that Michael had cowritten the script, she wondered if he'd had her in mind for the part from the beginning, especially since he'd claimed to regret their breakup. Oddly, she found satisfaction in the thought, though she would prefer to think she was wanted for her talents as an actress, not as a lover.

By the time she got to the hotel she was eager to tell Mason that she might have worked out a deal to finance his film. He was in the sitting room of their suite when she got there. One look and Dina could tell his day had not gone well.

Mason sat on the sofa, his stocking feet on the coffee table. He had a water glass half filled with Scotch in his hand. Lanks of tawny hair hung down over his forehead and he had a woebegone expression on his face.

Glancing over at her, he said, "I wish this town would go to bloody hell. They're bastards here. Every last one of them."

Dina put down her purse along with the script and went to sit next to him. She took his hand. "Didn't it go well at the studio?"

He gave a derisive laugh. "That bloody bastard Cavenaugh didn't even have the decency to come out of his hole to talk to me. He sent some twit to give me the brush-off. 'Mr. Cavenaugh's dealing with an emergency,' she says to me. 'I was the one who read the script anyway, so it's just as well we discuss it.' Discuss it, ha!"

"What did she say?"

"A lot of nothing. What it amounted to was that my film was too cerebral for the commercial audience. Cerebral! You'd think intelligence was a dirty word, for God's sake."

"You can't let one bad experience sour you on the project, darling," she said. "There are other producers."

"Thanks for being supportive, love," he said with a weak smile, "but you know and I know that's typical of the way people think in this town. It's no go."

"I'm ashamed of you for talking that way," Dina admonished. "It's never easy. Never. We have to find the right producer. Someone who shares your vision and your taste."

Mason leaned over and bussed her cheek. "You're a love. I don't often get down, but when I do I can always count on you to put a little starch in my backbone."

Dina squeezed his hand with both of hers. "It's no accident we're together."

He gave her a tired smile. "So, how was your day? I've been so busy complaining I've forgotten to ask."

"Interesting," she said. "I had an interesting day."

"Out with it. Are you cast as an Amazon shooting flaming arrows?"

"No. I've only glanced at the script, but it looks like the role is for a cop. But that's about all I know at this point. I need to read the entire script before I decide."

"Well, the way things are going with *Green September* I could hardly blame you for taking anything Cross offered. I'm afraid I'm proving to be a less than reliable partner." He took a big slug of Scotch.

"Don't be so hard on yourself, Mason. If I do this film with Michael, it could benefit us both."

He looked perplexed. "How so?"

Dina took a long breath. "Michael seems awfully eager to have me in his film—so much so that I might have leverage I wouldn't normally have."

"And?"

She squeezed his fingers hard. "I told him a condition for doing *Cold Hearts* was that he would have to help finance *Green September*. Michael has a lot of clout now that he has a couple of blockbusters under his belt. People will give him pretty much anything he wants."

"You made financing my film a condition of taking the role?"

"More or less."

Mason's eyes lit up. "And what did he say?"

"He's going to look at your script while I study his. I have to send him a copy this afternoon."

He leapt to his feet. "Darling, you're a genius! Where did you get that kind of influence with Cross that you could demand a thing like that?"

"It's not a done deal, Mason. Only a possibility. He has to like *Green September* and I have to like *Cold Hearts*."

"I shouldn't worry about that. The role can't be all that bad." He rubbed his hands together and started pacing, the way he always did when he was calculating. "A credit in a commercial hit can't hurt you. It proves you have range, for heaven's sake."

Dina folded her arms across her chest. "You know, you sound just like Sid Berman. What happened to the man who wants to make me an acclaimed actress of serious films?"

"What?" He turned to her. Obviously his mind was off exploring the possibilities of her scheme. "Sorry. I was thinking, love."

"You might be getting ahead of yourself. What if Michael doesn't like your script?" she countered, risking bringing him back to earth too suddenly.

"If Cross has any vision at all, he's bound to see merit in it. And if he's as keen on having you in his film as he seems to be, he's got to try to make mine work. I'll listen to any reasonable suggestions—so long as he doesn't try to destroy the bloody thing."

"But aren't you forgetting something? What if I don't like *Cold Hearts?* What if the part calls for making love in the trees while shooting flaming arrows, like you say? I may not take the role, regardless of what Michael offers."

Mason stopped pacing. A stricken look came over his face.

"You wouldn't want me to do anything stupid and tasteless, would you?" she said, certain he would instantly agree.

"I wouldn't want you doing something that would subject you to ridicule. But as I said, I don't see how you could lose, no matter what the role is like. It will be a hit."

"Mason, I can't believe you're saying that. You're not thinking of me. You're thinking of yourself."

He frowned and immediately returned to the sofa. As he dropped beside her, he put his arm around her shoulders. "I don't mean it that way, darling. *Green September* is not just my project, it's ours, love. You *are* Clarice.

If Cross wanted me to direct his film as a condition for financing mine, I'd do it in a flash. For you, Dina, as well as for me."

Mason was framing his argument in more palatable terms, but she still didn't like his attitude. Yet that wasn't really fair. The idea had been hers to begin with. She could hardly blame him for embracing it.

"Well, I don't want you to get your hopes up," she told him. "Talk is cheap, especially in Hollywood. It could fall through before it gets off the ground."

Mason pinched her cheek. "I have confidence in my script, darling," he said, "and I have confidence in you. If Michael Cross can be charmed, then you're the one to do it." He smiled. "Though it sounds like you might have done that already."

"You don't really mean that, Mason. Not seriously."

He looked thoroughly perplexed. "I don't mean what?"

"You wouldn't want me to . . . become involved with Michael just so we can make your damned film, would you?"

"Dina, whatever gave you that idea?"

"You just said—"

"I said you could charm him. There's nothing wrong in that. You told me only this morning that was how business was done here. Everybody's charming—or trying to charm—everybody else."

Dina was embarrassed to have jumped to conclusions. "I'm sorry, it's just that I thought you meant . . . something else."

Mason squeezed her body against his and she let her head rest on his shoulder. Everything seemed all right again. "I have to say, though, it's ruddy good luck Cross is so taken with you. How did this happen, anyway? You haven't said, have you? Was it *Mirabella* he saw you in, or *Sitting Pretty?*"

"Both. He said he liked me in both."

Mason shook his head. "How it is that people want to take a perfectly fine actress and dress her in a bikini and put a sword in her hand, is completely beyond me."

Dina was tempted to come right out and tell him the truth—to explain that she and Michael had a past—but Mason seemed so vulnerable just then that she couldn't be sure how he would take it. Besides, she wasn't in the mood for long explanations.

Mason was caressing her fingers and thinking—undoubtedly about *Green September.* Dina tried to think about it, too; about their future and the boost it might give to their careers. But Michael came sneaking into her mind—Michael, the man who'd told her he'd made a terrible mistake in letting her get away, the man who talked about the son they would have had by now, the man who all but said he wanted a relationship with her again.

Mason brushed a tendril of hair from her cheek. She shivered, but it wasn't from Mason's touch. It was because of the man occupying her mind, the man who, but for an odd twist of fate, might have been her husband at this very moment.

"Mason, can I ask you a hypothetical question?"

"Certainly. Anything you wish."

"What if Michael had a condition of his own? What if he refused to finance *Green September* unless I agreed to have an affair with him?"

Mason sat upright. "An affair?"

"Yes. Say he wanted me to sleep with him while we were working together on the film."

He gave her a hard look. "Dina, did Cross suggest something?"

"No. He flirted, of course, but everybody flirts. But he didn't proposition me."

"I'm relieved to hear that," Mason said. "For a moment there, you had me going.."

"What would you have said if he *had* propositioned me?" she asked. "You still haven't answered my question."

"I would have been offended. For your sake." He picked up his Scotch and drained it. "I'm going to get another. Can I bring you something?" He got up and went to the liquor cabinet.

"No, thanks. I had a margarita at lunch," she said.

Mason made no comment on that. Dina watched him pour himself a drink.

When he returned to the sofa and sat down beside her, she said, "Michael didn't proposition me, but I think he would try to seduce me if I gave him the slightest encouragement. I just thought you ought to know that before I send over a copy of your screenplay."

He gave her a sideways glance. "I'm not sure what kind of response you expect to that. There probably aren't ten straight men in California who wouldn't try to seduce you—given half a chance. It doesn't concern me unduly. I trust you." He sipped his Scotch. "But I would like to know what's prompted this."

Dina sighed. "I'm exploring your feelings for me, Mason. That's all."

He took her hand and pulled it to his lips, kissing her fingers. "I certainly hope I passed the test."

She smiled. If there was wistfulness in her expression, he failed to notice it. Still, she had only herself to blame. She'd been deliberately coy. Besides, if anyone was really at fault, it was Michael. But that was all right, she'd gotten him out of her system. Mason and their evening together was what counted now.

"Well?" he said, when she hadn't answered. "How did I do?"

"You passed the test," she said. "With flying colors."

"Marvelous," he said. "Now that's settled, the next order of business is planning dinner. We really must celebrate your cleverness."

"If you want Michael to produce your film, the next order of business ought to be to send him a copy of the screenplay. I promised I'd get one to him this afternoon."

Mason got to his feet. "By all means."

Dina smiled at his eagerness. "While you find a copy, I'll telephone the front desk and ask them to arrange for a courier."

"Righto. Mustn't neglect our dear friend, Mr. Cross." He disappeared into his bedroom.

Dina got up and went to the phone. While she was talking to the clerk, Mason returned to the sitting room. He put a copy of the script beside her and stood there. When she'd hung up, he kissed her lightly on her ear.

"If Mr. Cross wants an affair with you, he can't have one," he whispered. "I'd allow a spot of flirting, but that's my best offer."

Dina's lips curved into a smile. "I'll tell him that, should it come up," she said.

What she dared not add was that even flirting with Michael Cross could be a fatal mistake.

3

OVER THE NEXT THREE DAYS, Dina spent much of her time regretting having gotten involved with Michael again. No matter how often she told herself it was only business—something she was doing for Mason's sake—the potential problems were already apparent.

First, she caught herself thinking about Michael even when she was with Mason. That was not a good sign. Second, Mason had already convinced himself that the deal would work out, making it difficult to impossible for her to pull out. Finally, and worst of all, she worried about playing the role. Her character was supposed to be an old lover of Michael's character, and that hit a little too close to home. Even worse, there were two major love scenes in the script and she had no illusions about where that could end up.

Dina was confident she'd ultimately handle the situation but didn't relish the struggle. There was no doubt that Michael wanted to tempt her—he'd all but admitted he still wanted her—if only to prove to himself that he could have her again if he wished.

Fortunately, the ball was in Michael's court now and she was fairly certain he'd make his move before the weekend. But what if he decided to do *Green September*? She'd be trapped, forced to do *Cold Hearts*.

Her last hope was to try to convince Mason to pursue other options. She'd asked him to read the script. He'd gone over it that morning and they agreed to discuss it after their tennis game.

"What about my character, what do you think of her?" she'd asked as he stretched out on the sofa in their sitting room. He was still wearing his tennis clothes.

He thought for a moment. "I've certainly seen worse. Cross is right, the part does have some meat to it."

"You're suggesting I ought to accept it," she said, disheartened.

"It can't do you any harm," he said. "Not like *Revenge of the Ghouls*."

She took off her headband and began twirling it. "Mason, I don't want to avoid harm. I only want to take roles that will do my career some good."

"I think Sid is right," he said, sitting up. "This will be a good opportunity for you to get exposure. You're fortunate Cross wants you for it."

Dina wanted so badly to tell him the truth, to let him know what he was asking her to do. But to Mason it was just another role. Love scenes were things that actresses sometimes did, that's all.

"I haven't decided how I feel about the nudity," she said. "I haven't so much as exposed a breast before."

Mason chuckled. "Darling, we're not talking porn. Cross needs an R rating. A glimpse of your body, some titillation, that's all they can get away with."

She was miffed. Mason refused to see the problem in personal terms. To him she was just an actress, *Cold Hearts* just a film, and Michael Cross just an actor. But she was beginning to see that to Mason, her taking the part was more than just a role—it was his meal ticket.

Dina set her headband down on the coffee table and began pacing. Mason watched her.

"Darling," he said, "what's bothering you? You haven't been yourself the past few days."

She stopped pacing and looked at him. She was tempted to tell him. "There's a lot hanging in the balance, and I'd hate for us to be used."

"What do you mean, 'used'?"

She hesitated. The words were ready to come out—*Michael's got ulterior motives,* she wanted to say. *He sees this project as an opportunity to take advantage of me. Michael and I were lovers once. What he really wants is to seduce me!*

"Dina, what do you mean, 'used'?" Mason said again.

"Oh, nothing in particular," she finally replied. "Just Hollywood. The same old thing."

"God knows, I complain about the place myself, but truth be known, they couldn't hang us if we didn't risk putting our head in the noose."

"Yes, you're right," she said wearily. "I should be grateful for the opportunities I've had."

The telephone rang and Mason got up to answer it. "Must be destiny calling," he said jauntily. He picked up the receiver. "Fellows." He listened. "Cross, old man," he said airily. He turned and grinned. "Dina and I were just discussing your film.... That's right.... She wanted me to read the script. Hope you don't mind.... I was rather impressed, to be frank. Dina thinks playing Alice would be a fabulous opportunity. I couldn't agree more."

Mason winked at her. "But I should let her speak for herself, shouldn't I?"

She found Mason's attempt to ingratiate himself annoying. It would have been far more gratifying if he'd been jealous or resentful.

"So have you had a chance to look over *Green September* yet?" Mason asked.

Dina watched his brows rise with delight.

"Interest has to come first, doesn't it, old man?" he said. He nodded as he listened. "We'd be delighted to meet with you, Michael. Name the time and place.... Tomorrow evening would be lovely, I'm sure." He glanced in Dina's direction, but didn't wait for a sign. "Your place at seven. Perfect.... Yes, good talking to you. Look forward to meeting you, Michael."

Mason hung up the phone and gave an uncharacteristic shout of joy. "He's interested in talking about *Green September!*" he cried, thrusting his fist into the air. "Yes!"

"He is?" Dina heard the disappointment in her voice. "He actually likes *Green September?*"

"He wants to discuss it. That's a first step. I'm sure he doesn't want to sound too enthusiastic. Cross's background is in the theater, isn't it? He must know quality writing when he sees it."

"I wouldn't jump to conclusions, Mason."

A frown clouded his face. "What do you mean, darling? You don't think he's serious?"

"I don't know. It's possible he's playing us along."

"What for?"

She sighed. "There's no point in idle speculation. Let's wait and see what Michael says. *And* what he wants."

"I'm an optimist by nature, Dina. You know that perfectly well." He paced back and forth, happy with excitement.

Dina felt her stomach knot. This was what she'd wanted for Mason from the start, but dammit, it wasn't as satisfying as it should have been. Why? she wondered. What was she afraid of? Maybe it was the way Mason was reacting. It would have been so much better if he'd been wary, like most other men. But then, maybe it was her fault for withholding the truth about Michael. She hoped she wouldn't end up regretting it more than she already did.

WHILE HE WAITED for Dina and Mason to arrive, Michael Cross leaned back in his cream leather chair, his feet propped up on the ottoman. He was wearing white jeans and a V-neck cashmere sweater that was a blue a few shades darker than his eyes. He ran his hand back through his still damp hair, then flipped through Fellows's screenplay, trying to decide what was wrong with it.

There were obvious problems—Fellows focused on character at the expense of plot and the writing was far too introspective. That worked in the novel, but it wouldn't in film. Changes would have to be made. Fortunately the setting and period were good—eighteenth-century France. *Valmont,* another film in that time frame and setting, had done well at the box office, but it had been loaded with intrigue.

Green September, on the other hand, was about the daughter of a disgraced nobleman and her ill-fated affair with the son of the man who ruined her father. It was a straightforward tale—passionate, poignant and bittersweet—not all that different from *Romeo and Juliet*.

But love stories had always been a staple of the film industry. If the chemistry between the two leads was good, and Fellows agreed to a few of his suggestions, they might just pull it off.

The question was, how did he tell Mason that without alienating him? Normally it wouldn't matter if he did offend him, but there was more at stake here than just a filmmaker's ego. Dina was an issue, as well.

From the very beginning he hadn't liked the conditions she'd set for doing *Cold Hearts*, but it had become apparent that it was the only way to get her under contract. Dina had him right where she wanted him—assuming he couldn't live without having her in his picture. And he couldn't.

For him, there could be no other Alice, it was as simple as that. Casting her had been easy. The hard part was figuring out how to get her to take the role.

He worried that Dina would be uncomfortable doing Alice. Her character had once been the lover of his character, and that might put her off. But the director in him was equally sure it could make for some wonderful acting.

Like *Green September*, the storyline of *Cold Hearts* was simple, but it was laced with plenty of action. Alice was a city cop in charge of an investigation into a drug smuggling ring. He would play her old lover, a DEA agent who comes to town and takes charge of the case. When they go undercover, posing as lovers, the sexual tension between them would mirror their tension over who should head the case. Add a bunch of bad guys who were into martial arts, a major explosion at a warehouse by the docks, and the sinking of the ship carrying the contraband, and you had another Michael Cross action-thriller.

Cold Hearts would be his first film that had a love story for a subplot and he could not imagine any actress but Dina in the role. But there was so much history between them, and not all of it was pleasant.

He'd been bitter after Dina had left him. Wounded, definitely. And heartbroken—even though he'd refused to admit it, even to himself. Ego and pride had demanded she come back to him, not that he go to her.

In the early days after their breakup, when she'd steadfastly maintained her silence, he assumed it was because she'd felt she'd outgrown him. Then, when his film career had been successful beyond his wildest dreams, he'd half expected to hear from her. The call never came.

By then her Oscar triumph had been sullied by several failures at the box office and she'd gone off to England to lick her wounds. He'd feared then that she was too embarrassed to reach out to him because his star had eclipsed hers. So he'd waited, biding his time until an opportunity to contact her presented itself.

Now that he'd finally engineered an encounter, a new problem had arisen. Fellows had popped up right in the middle of things and was turning out to be more than a minor irritant. Michael wasn't quite sure how to take her talk of marriage. He didn't know the Englishman, but from what he'd heard, he didn't think Mason was Dina's type. What she was doing with the guy was beyond him.

If he'd learned anything the other day at lunch, it was that Dina hadn't forgotten him. There had been vibrations. And she'd been just as aware of it as he. Yet whatever her true feelings were, she hadn't wavered in her commitment to Fellows. She seemed determined to stand by him.

If that was really what she wanted, there wasn't a lot he could do about it. But he could test her. He could find out how strong the commitment was. She would have to prove it to him that there was nothing left in her heart for him.

Michael glanced at his watch. He had half an hour before they'd arrive. It was already twilight. From where he sat he could see the lights of the city beginning to twinkle in the hazy panorama stretching from the Pacific to Beverly Hills. The falling night distracted him.

Tossing Fellows's script aside, he stepped outside to the patio. The air was fragrant with the smells of autumn. L.A. was not northern Indiana, where he'd been born, but once in a while he'd catch a scent that reminded him of Indiana and his childhood there, of the years before he fell in love with the stage and headed for New York to learn his craft. He took a deep breath, savoring those memories of his boyhood.

Though it was relatively warm for October, something about this particular evening took him back, not to La Porte, Indiana, but to the green hillsides of Seattle and the sweet, heartrending days he'd spent with Dina.

Over the past five years he'd frequently thought of their life together, of the way things had once been. In retrospect it seemed a perfect existence—struggling young actors without a concern in the world but each other and their work in the theater.

Dina—tall, shapely, with lush ebony hair and perfect white skin—would always be the love of his life. He had no doubt about that. Whatever else happened, whoever else came along, it would always be Dina.

So often he'd yearned to look into her dove gray eyes, to kiss her mouth. There'd been many lonely evenings when he'd craved her company. Geraldine Winterhalter, the witty comedienne, full of enthusiasm, laughing, happy, thrilled by life. She'd been his. And he'd lost her.

Whenever he thought back to those days in Seattle he would picture Dina in the morning, her body wrapped in a tattered terry robe. She was so real, so human. Dina was the sexiest, most endearing woman alive. Being with her had been one hell of an adventure.

He went down the steps to the lower terrace where the pool lay still under the charcoal sky, tinged in the west by rose and amber hues. Los Angeles lay spread out before him, but it was the milky haze of Puget Sound he longed for, and life with Dina. Though he'd never quite been able to get enough of her then, he realized, now, that he hadn't truly appreciated what he'd had. Was it too late? Were those days, and the possibility of others like them, gone forever?

He made a slow circuit of the lawn. He was rich and successful, but he was a lonely man and he knew it. There'd been women in his life, true, but as charming and clever and lovely as they were, none could fill the void that Dina had left. He'd tried to form a meaningful connection with someone, but had gone from one relationship to another until he grew tired of the game. That was when he knew he had to try once more with her.

Checking the time again, he went inside to get ready. Dina had liked the cheap cologne he'd worn in the early days and so, in a fit of whimsy, he'd gone out and bought a bottle—for old times' sake.

He couldn't be sure what the scent of it would do to her, but it had already had its effect on him. One whiff had flooded him with memories. The time she'd gotten tipsy on champagne and smeared his body with the cologne from head to toe before they'd made love. Or the time she'd sprinkled a few drops on her pillow so that she could dream about him when he'd made that trip to New York. Then, when he'd called her, she'd told him she'd awakened aroused and moist and wanting him. It was all he could do to keep from getting on a plane that night.

And when he returned to Seattle, Dina had picked him up at the airport in a borrowed van. In back was a mattress, candles, an ice bucket with cheap champagne. She'd parked in the short-term lot, but they spent two hours making love anyway, with the jets taking off and landing practically over their heads.

He sighed. It had been a romance of the ages. The question was, could it be again?

DURING THE DRIVE over to Michael's place, Dina noticed that Mason was as nervous as she. He'd put up a brave front, but the bottom line was, Mason had had doubts from the start how well he could play the Hollywood game, and the difficulties he'd had in getting *Green September* off the ground had only added to his fears. Still, doubts or not, he seemed determined to give it his best shot, and she was proud of him for that. Her only regret was that his best hope was Michael Cross.

She took Mason's arm as the chauffeur drove up the twisting road to Michael's estate. "If for some reason this doesn't work out tonight," she said softly, "I want to get on a plane tomorrow for London."

"Oh, it'll work out," Mason said with more assurance than he probably felt. "The only question is how much bloody damage he'll do to my film in the process. It seems everybody involved has got to put their stamp on the project. I'm damned sure Cross won't be any different."

"Well, don't give more than you feel comfortable with," she said.

Mason looked at her. "Dina, you almost sound like you don't want me to do the deal."

"I don't want it to be a miserable experience for you."

"It all depends on what's in his head, doesn't it? And I suppose we'll find out what that is soon enough." He patted her knee and looked out the window.

Dina decided, right then, that she'd rather give up her career than see Mason humiliated. Better they go back to England and do TV films for the BBC. Better she do theater in the West End than prostitute herself for Hollywood financing.

As they entered the gate to Michael's estate, Dina took a deep breath. The chauffeur helped them out of the limousine and the housekeeper who had served lunch the other day opened the front door.

"Mr. Cross is on the telephone," she said, ushering them into the library. "He asked me to fix you a drink and tell you he'll be with you shortly."

The room had books floor to ceiling on two walls. There was a bar on the third wall. The fourth was entirely of glass and overlooked the city. Mason glanced around before heading for one of the two cream leather sofas that dominated the space. Dina followed him and sat close beside him.

"What may I serve you?" the woman asked from the bar.

"Scotch whiskey, neat, for me," Mason replied. "What would you like, love?" he asked Dina.

"Mineral water, if you have it," she said.

While the housekeeper began fixing their drinks, Dina and Mason exchanged looks. They gave each other nervous smiles.

"Quite a spread Cross has here," Mason said under his breath. "Is he flamboyant, as well?"

"I wouldn't call Michael flamboyant."

"How would you describe him?"

Dina didn't know how to answer—the adjectives that immediately came to mind were entirely inappropriate. "Michael has a certain confidence without being pushy," she finally said. "And he can be . . . direct."

"He's not a bullshitter, then?"

"No."

The housekeeper brought them their drinks and put a bowl of nuts on the table. Then she left the room. Mason quaffed half his Scotch in one long swallow. He put down his glass. "Bloody nuisance, crawling to people and begging for money."

"Artists have done that for hundreds of years. There's no reason to expect things to be any different now. It's the price of being a creative person. There are so few who really have it made. People like Michael, I mean."

"I'll cherish the day they have to come crawling to me," Mason said, popping a nut into his mouth. "Do you suppose Cross appreciates what he's got?"

"I expect so. Michael's paid his dues. But ask him, if you really want to know. He'll tell you."

Mason gave her an inquisitive look. "For having done a little theater with the guy, you seem to know what makes him tick. How friendly were the two of you, anyway?"

There was more curiosity than suspicion in Mason's voice. Dina was sorry he'd asked, because she didn't want to lie. "I know him well enough to know how he thinks, believe me."

He grinned. "I'm pretty damned fortunate to have you on my side, aren't I?"

"Are you?"

He squeezed her hand and picked up his glass. "Does the bloke have taste? That's the critical question, wouldn't you say?"

Dina watched him take another slug of Scotch. "I would say he does. Michael's talented and bright. And he has integrity. At least, he did when I knew him."

She wondered why she was speaking of him so charitably when for days she'd been wary, apprehensive. Maybe it was because in her memories Michael wasn't threatening. It was a different story when she was around him, though. Since their lunch she'd prayed he'd taken her lecture to heart, accepted the fact that Mason was the man in her life now.

Mason finished off his drink and put down the empty glass. "Let's hope Hollywood hasn't corrupted him," he said under his breath.

Dina nodded. "Yes, let's hope."

Michael suddenly appeared at the door. "My apologies. Sorry not to greet you when you arrived."

His casual, comfortable and confident good looks jumped right out at her as he stepped into the room.

Mason was on his feet. Michael extended his hand. "We meet at last, Mason. Always good to know people whose work you admire."

They shook hands.

Dina got up as well, offering her hand. Michael took it, but immediately leaned over to kiss her cheek. "Don't you look lovely this evening," he said.

His cologne enveloped her. It was delicious, and oh so familiar, despite the years. He smelled like the Michael she'd known, different than the other day at lunch. His scent got her in the gut, viscerally, as smells always did. She'd once liked it so much that she'd sprinkled a little on the bathrobe he'd kept at her apartment. That way she could wear it on nights he wasn't there and feel close to him.

The look in his eye told her he knew she'd noticed, and that he'd worn it intentionally, hoping she'd remember. What a bastard. He was pulling out all the stops.

He turned to Mason. "You both look so nice, I almost feel like I should go in and put on a tie. I did say super casual, didn't I?"

Mason had on one of his tweedy sports coats. She'd worn silk pants and a silk shirt, both in a soft rose color.

"Our common language and common culture aren't so common," Mason replied.

"You're right," Michael said with a laugh. "In California, 'super casual' means one step up from naked." He gave Dina a wink and slapped Mason on the shoulder. "Take off your jacket and tie if you'd feel more comfortable."

Mason did take off his coat, though Dina knew he'd have preferred to keep it on.

"I see you've gotten drinks. Sit down and make yourselves at home while I get myself one." Before walking to the bar, he noticed Mason looking at his empty glass. "Can I freshen that for you, old bean?" He gave Dina a sly grin while Mason handed the glass to him.

"Thanks ever so."

"Scotch?"

"Please."

"How are you doing, Dina? Can I bring you something?"

She hadn't yet touched her water. "I'm fine." She watched Michael go to the bar. "Sounds like you've been watching some old British films, old bean," she quipped.

He laughed. "I try to make my guests feel at home." He took a bottle from the shelf. "Actually, I watched *Mirabella* again this afternoon," he said, as he poured some whiskey into Mason's glass.

"Did you?" Mason said, brightening.

"Yes, and as I told you on the phone, there were things about the film I liked a lot. I think the critics were unfair."

"The moviegoing public wasn't any more generous," Mason said. "But Dina was awfully good. Saved the bloody thing, really."

"Dina brings a lot to the screen," Michael said. "I'm her biggest fan, I'm sure."

She gave him a look. "I hope you two don't intend to spend the evening flattering me. There are far more important things to discuss." She smiled. "Though there's never been an actress who didn't thrive on a little sincere flattery."

Michael returned with a glass in each hand. After handing Mason his, he dropped onto the sofa across from them. "I think we should drink to sincere flattery. What do you say, Mason?"

"By all means." He saluted each of them with his glass. "Cheers." Then he took a big slug of his Scotch.

Michael was looking at her the way he had at lunch, though in deference to Mason he didn't hold his gaze quite as long. He shifted his eyes to Mason, who'd set his glass down and grabbed a few nuts.

"Seriously, Mason," he said, "I'm interested in *Green September*, mainly because there was much I admired in *Mirabella*."

"Are we talking about Dina or something else?" Mason asked with a crooked grin.

"Oh, stop," she chided, nudging him with her elbow.

Mason took her hand and kissed it. "Darling, no man can resist a beautiful, talented actress, no matter who she's playing opposite. Am I right, Cross?"

"Absolutely."

"Okay," she said. "Enough teasing. Let's talk about *Green September* and *Cold Hearts*. I don't want to sit through drinks and dinner with business hanging over my head. If we get it out of the way first, we can enjoy the evening—which I'm sure we'll manage to do regardless of how things turn out."

"Dina, love," Mason said, "let's get at least one drink down the man's throat before we get serious. Can't allow him an unfair advantage now, can we?"

Michael nodded. "I can see it's that feisty impatience in the American female that attracted you to her, Mason."

"You American chaps find it tedious, do you?" Mason said, playing along.

"No, actually we like it. Helps to propagate the race."

"I wish you two would stop bantering and start talking about the film. I'm serious about not wanting to play cat and mouse all evening."

"All right, Lady Winterhalter," Michael said, leaning back and crossing his legs. "Your opinions are as critical as anyone else's. Why don't you tell us what you think of Alice and *Cold Hearts?*"

"All right," she said, drawing a deep breath. Michael and Mason both sipped their drinks as she gathered her thoughts. "I was impressed with the script. I like Alice. My reservations are about the way you intend to handle the sex scenes."

"Oh, I'm a firm believer in safe sex."

He laughed and winked at Mason, who joined in. Dina colored, as much with annoyance as embarrassment. "I'd assumed we'd be using body doubles, Michael."

"No, sexual chemistry is essentially psychological. It's as much in the eyes as the limbs, Dina. I want your body, not anyone else's."

She turned an even deeper shade of red and quickly picked up her glass. "You mean figuratively speaking, of course," she murmured.

"Of course."

"Seriously," she said, "I'd like to know that the sex scenes will be tasteful. Subtlety is sexier anyway, in my opinion."

"When it comes to sex," he said, "I aim to please...."

Her eyes narrowed.

"The audience," he added quickly. "And yes, I do agree that subtlety is key." He sipped his drink, watching her.

"What sort of time frame are we looking at?" she asked. "When do you plan to start shooting?"

"That's the problem. We're already well into preproduction. I'd like to start shooting on location in a week."

"A week? Isn't that a little quick? What will you do if we can't come to an agreement? Do you have somebody else waiting in the wings?"

"No, I've been counting on your good judgment."

She took another sip of water. "You realize, of course, that by exposing your desperation, you're giving me leverage."

"I'm counting on your compassion."

She glanced at Mason, who'd been listening quietly. "When did compassion ever count for anything in this business?"

"I'd like to think I'm among friends," Michael replied.

"*I'm* treating this like a business deal," she said. "I won't be ruthless, but I won't compromise, either."

Michael contemplated her, nodding. "All right, let's get to the bottom line."

"My final consent to do the film depends on what you're going to do about *Green September*."

"You'll only take the part if I can arrange the financing for Mason's film. Is that what I'm hearing?"

"Yes."

"So Mason and I have to strike our deal before you and I can make ours."

Dina nodded. "If we can't work something out on *Green September* I plan to leave at once for London, so I won't be available to do your picture."

He rubbed his chin. "I appreciate your honesty." He turned to Mason, who shifted uncomfortably. "If I can raise the money, I'll produce your film," he said, "but I, too, have conditions. You'll have to be able to live with them, or there's no point in going on."

"What are they?" Mason reached for his glass with a trembling hand.

"I'll have the final say on casting and budget. You'll have artistic control, except for instances where there are conflicts directly impacting casting and budget."

"I have the major parts cast. Dina will play Clarice, and Rob Sharp has verbally agreed to play Stephen—provided there's no conflict in his schedule."

"Both good choices," Michael said.

"I won't do the picture without Dina. This film's hers as much as it is mine."

Michael thought for a moment. "Okay, Dina's in for sure, but I want to talk to Rob. I know him fairly well. Leave that part of it to me."

Mason was silent. Michael glanced at Dina, who'd been holding her tongue, letting Mason speak for him-

self. He could make his own decisions, and she didn't
want him feeling any pressure because of her.

"Do whatever you think best," she told him when he
caught her eye. "I don't want you feeling any obligation
to me. This is your project, you're in control."

"You're Clarice as far as I'm concerned," he said.
"That's nonnegotiable."

"I won't ram a cast down your throat, Mason," Michael said. "I'll consult with you. I have no problem with
that. But if there's any disagreement, the final decision
has to be mine."

Mason drained the last of his second Scotch. Dina
could tell he was hating every minute of this. He de-
tested the business end of things and wanted nothing but
to make his film.

"How soon will you know about the financing?" he
asked.

"I'll have to make a few phone calls. If I can get ahold
of the people I need, I could have an answer as early as
tomorrow or the day after."

That seemed to raise his spirits. "That quick?"

"I'm no smarter now than when I was poor," Michael
said, "but the rest of the world doesn't seem to know that.
Of course, one stupid mistake and I'm garbage—the
same as anyone else in this town. We're all only as good
as our last movie, right?"

"Don't remind me," Dina said under her breath.

But Michael heard. "Flops needn't be fatal. Just so-
bering."

"I'm sober as a church mouse."

He grinned. Dina remembered that grin and hated him
for using it on her now, when she was feeling so shaky.

She turned to Mason. He was preoccupied, oblivious to the sexual undercurrents flowing back and forth.

"Then, if I understand you, Cross," Mason said, "you're taking a risk on this, too."

"For starters, I'll have to put a few million of my own in it to demonstrate to my investors that I have the courage of my convictions." He glanced at Dina, his eyes telling her that his "convictions" involved more than just money.

She tried to relax, but her heart was pounding. She could feel the tension, knowing that Mason was agonizing. Casting was always important to him. It was to almost any director. But he also knew that all he had to do was say yes and he could probably be sure that his picture got made.

The housekeeper entered with a tray of hors d'oeuvres, which she put on the low glass table between them. "Dinner in half an hour, Mr. Cross. Can I bring you anything else?"

"Mr. Fellows could use another drink," he replied.

Mason handed her his glass. Then, rubbing his chin, he asked, "Do you have anyone else in mind for Stephen?"

"Rob's not a bad choice at all. I don't want to give you that impression. But I do want to give it some thought and, as I say, talk to him."

"When could we start preproduction?" Mason asked, plucking a canapé from the tray. "I've been ready personally for a couple of months."

"Assuming we're all agreed, Dina and I will be busy for three or four weeks shooting *Cold Hearts*. I'll probably need her for a day or two now and then after that, but generally speaking she's yours as soon after we wrap as she wants."

"I'll have no problem doing the films back to back," she said. She turned to Mason. "I'll be with you in London in a month at the latest."

He beamed. "I can use the time to take care of preproduction and pull together the crew. I have a place in France in mind for the location shooting. I can be set up and ready to go when Dina and Rob arrive." He leaned forward and rubbed his hands together. "This could all work out rather nicely."

The housekeeper brought Mason his drink and left the room. Mason took a distracted sip.

"I'm warming to the idea," he said, sounding almost giddy.

Michael gave Dina a smile. "Is it time to have some champagne opened?"

He was playing it cool, but there was triumph in his eyes. And now, having heard the schedule, she suddenly understood. Michael, damn him, was getting her for a month, and getting rid of Mason at the same time! The bastard was clever *and* shrewd. But he didn't know her as well as he thought—not the woman she had become. Dina slipped her arm through Mason's.

"Playing Clarice for Mason is my fondest dream," she said sweetly.

"And having you play Alice for me has been *my* fondest dream," he replied. "So, if we're all as pleased as we seem, why don't I call for that champagne?"

Mason popped another canapé in his mouth, holding up a finger as he chewed. "Don't forget your investors, Cross," he said. "We bloody well need them."

"At this stage, I consider that a mere technicality." Michael winked at Dina, who pressed herself against Mason's arm.

Both men seemed in a festive mood, the tension of the negotiation over. She wanted it to be a cause for celebration, but a part of her wasn't sure just what to think. Had she and Mason pulled off a coup, or had they made a terrible mistake? Only time would tell.

4

DINA AWOKE AS MASON climbed from the bed and staggered off toward the bathroom. He was naked and the morning sun made his pale skin appear especially pasty. The poor thing was obviously suffering. Thanks to the Scotch and the champagne, he'd nearly passed out on the way home.

She'd been embarrassed for him. And for herself. It was not the image she'd wanted to present to Michael. But then, why should she give a damn what Michael thought? Mason only drank too much when he was under stress. That didn't justify it, of course, but he was usually much more controlled. Besides, she knew the kind of person he really was and that was all that counted.

After a minute or two Mason returned from the bath, dropping heavily onto the bed. He pulled the sheet up, then rolled his head toward her.

"Good morning, darling," he croaked.

"How do you feel?"

"Like hell. Sorry. I hope I wasn't too much of a sod."

"You were, but that's all right. I forgive you."

He pulled her hand to his mouth and kissed it. "You're an angel, Dina. I don't deserve you."

"Let's not get melodramatic."

"You're right. Stiff upper lip. I've got a ruddy reputation to maintain." He smiled weakly. "Tell me, how is it that you're in my bed? Was it your idea or mine?"

"It was mutual."

"I expect I insisted."

"Sort of," she said.

"But I didn't perform, did I?"

"You were affectionate, Mason."

He shook his head with disgust. "I didn't think so. What a terrible waste. Here I am, with the most beautiful woman in the world, a glorious reason to celebrate, and I can't get the bloody thing up!"

"Today is a new day. Yesterday wasn't our last."

He caressed her cheek with his finger. "It's terrible to blow an opportunity, though. How many do we have in a lifetime?" He groaned. "I must give up drink. Don't let me have another, ever!"

"It's up to you, Mason. Not me."

He sighed. "I know. I'll be better. I promise." He kissed her fingers again and lay silently staring at the ceiling. "So, what do you think, love? Am I going to get to do my film or am I not?"

"Michael certainly seemed optimistic."

"You don't think it was puff, then?"

"No, I don't think that's his style."

Mason sighed again. "God, I hope you're right."

They fell into a contemplative silence. Dina thought back on the previous evening. Dinner had gone well. Mason had consumed a lot of champagne. By the time they'd indulged in wine and after-dinner drinks, he was pretty well out of it. From that point the conversation had been mainly between her and Michael.

They'd talked about the film business. They'd talked about England. They talked about theater. Dina carefully steered the conversation away from the past. It wasn't until they'd loaded Mason into the limousine and were saying goodbye that the conversation became more personal.

"I'm looking forward to working with you, Dina," he'd said as they stood by the limo, under the stars. "I'm glad everything has fallen into place."

"You seem to have had it all planned."

"Perhaps."

"And pretty much gotten your way."

"I won't deny it," he'd said.

"Don't make the mistake of overplaying your hand, Michael."

He'd looked into her eyes. "Meaning?"

"It was clever of you to schedule things so that Mason will be off in Europe, while I'm here with you."

"I don't like distractions on the set. I prefer not to have wives, husbands, children, lovers or pets around. I want my actors to concentrate on each other."

"Presumably, you mean while working."

"Yes, while working," he'd replied.

She'd stared at him as he'd stared at her. "I want your promise that you won't try to take advantage of the situation."

"What situation?"

"Me being with you, while Mason's away."

He'd smiled, looking guilty, but not too guilty. "We've already made our deal. I won't accept additional conditions after the fact."

"It's not too late for me to back out," she'd warned.

"Anything that happens will happen because you want it to. If you trust yourself, you have no reason to worry."

"That almost sounds like a challenge."

"It's not meant to be. It's simply a fact."

"Can I count on you respecting my wishes?" she'd asked.

"Your wish is my command."

She'd repressed a smile. "So long as you remember that it's not the other way around, we should be all right."

"I mean to please, Dina."

She'd looked in the limo at Mason whose head was thrown back against the seat. He was already suffering. And also oblivious to what was going on. She turned back to Michael. "I'd better go."

She'd extended her hand, letting him know that it was all she would allow. Michael reciprocated.

"Now let's hope your financing comes through," she'd said. "It would be awful if we went through all this for nothing."

"I got to see you again," he'd said, giving a little shrug. "That's hardly nothing."

She'd shaken her head. "Don't, Michael. Don't even think that way."

"You can limit my actions," he'd said, "but not my dreams and desires."

She'd turned then, and climbed into the limousine. She was trembling as they drove off.

"Do you think Cross will call today?" Mason asked, interrupting her reverie. "Or will he keep me dangling until tomorrow?"

"Michael has no desire to see you dangle, Mason, I'm quite sure." *What he wants is to see you gone*, she thought cynically.

How sad it was that she'd let herself get caught up in a conspiracy against the man she loved. Michael was manipulating Mason and she was being forced to stand idly by—watching, knowing exactly what was going on. And she could do nothing about it, nothing at all but keep her own house in order. That had become her chief obligation: to remain true to Mason.

MICHAEL DROVE HIS Jaguar along Sunset Boulevard, toward Bel Air. He was still west of the San Diego Freeway and running late. Mal Bernstein had backed out of the *Green September* deal that morning after giving a tentative go the day before. Now Michael was left two million short. He couldn't get the other investors to make up the shortfall, so he'd had to commit the extra money himself. The opportunity to spend some time with Dina was getting to be an expensive proposition.

Michael sighed. What the hell, it was only money. If the day came when he ran out and couldn't make more, he'd live without it. It sounded rather facile, he knew, but having that attitude was liberating. It was terrible the way people with a few bucks lived in mortal fear of losing it. If he was afraid of anything now, it was of losing Dina forever.

The traffic slowed as he neared the freeway. He glanced at his watch. Wouldn't it be ironic if in his haste to put together his financing package so that he could pack Mason off to merry old England, he ended up making the poor bastard miss his plane? And if traffic on the way to the airport was as bad as this, that just might happen.

He grabbed the phone and dialed the Bel Air Hotel. He asked for Mason Fellows, but it was Dina who answered.

"I'm running late," he said. "I got tied up."

"Maybe Mason and I should take a cab," she replied.

"Well, I can probably get there as fast as a taxi, so I'm your best bet. If you could be waiting in the lobby, it would save a few minutes."

"Mason's packed and ready. We'll go now."

"Is he still as excited about the financing coming through as he was last night?"

"Ecstatic," she said with unguarded enthusiasm. "He's been blocking scenes all morning."

"If it had been me, I'd have spent the morning saying goodbye to you. Properly."

There was a long silence and he realized he'd said the wrong thing. Dina had been defensive about Mason from the first. He'd told himself a thousand times that it was important that he take things slowly, that he put her at ease. But dammit, that was hard.

"Well, I suppose everybody has their own way of doing things, don't they?" he added lamely.

"You may as well know I wasn't pleased when you offered to drive Mason to the airport. If you'd been at all considerate, Michael, you'd have known we'd rather be alone."

"I didn't twist his arm. I offered and he accepted."

"You took advantage of Mason."

"If you're that offended, I can wait in the car while you see him off."

"Maybe that wouldn't be such a bad idea."

Michael smiled to himself. It wasn't seeing Mason Fellows off that interested him, it was driving Dina back afterward. They needed to discuss *Cold Hearts,* but more than that, he wanted to see how she'd react to him once Fellows was physically removed from the scene.

"I'm crossing the San Diego Freeway now," he said. "You'd better head for the lobby."

"All right."

"See you in a few minutes."

Michael hung up the phone and smiled. In a couple of hours he'd have her to himself. But would it be a victory or not?

Minutes later he was passing U.C.L.A. on the right. At the far edge of the campus he turned left, entering Bel Air. Mason and Dina were standing outside the hotel as he swung the Jaguar up to the entrance.

Dina was in a violet suit that looked stunning with her dark hair. Mason was predictably tweedy, almost handsome in his peculiar way. The poor fellow had been embarrassed about his drinking the other night and had apologized profusely when he'd called the next day to discuss financing. God knows, it would have been fine with him if Fellows was dead drunk all the time—at least when he was with Dina. Michael still hadn't allowed himself to dwell on the thought of them being together.

While Mason supervised the loading of his luggage and tipped the doorman, Dina climbed into the back seat. "Hello, Michael," she said in a neutral tone. There was neither warmth nor coolness in her voice.

"You look great."

"Thank you."

"I hope my lateness didn't create a problem."

"We'll survive, I'm sure."

He noticed a touch of sarcasm in her voice. She was looking out the window and not at him. Mason came to the passenger door.

"Off we go!" he said cheerily as he climbed in. He reached over to shake Michael's hand. "Awfully kind of you to give us a lift, old man."

"My pleasure, Mason," he said, starting the car. "It's important to be on good terms with the people I work with." He glanced in the rearview mirror and caught Dina's eye. Immediately she looked away.

The traffic on the San Diego Freeway wasn't bad and they made the trip in good time. Mason talked most of the way about his plans for *Green September*. Michael paid only enough attention to be polite. His mind was on Dina, who seemed unusually subdued.

They arrived at the terminal building with twenty minutes to spare. He let them off, then went to park the car, saying he'd meet them at the gate. By the time he got there the passengers were already boarding. Dina and Mason were standing by the ramp, holding hands and looking into each other's eyes.

He stopped some distance away to give them a little privacy. There seemed to be genuine affection between them. Fellows was a decent guy, likable even, once you got used to him. At least he wasn't plastic and shallow, like so much of Hollywood. And when he was sober, he could be both witty and incisive. He had talent. But Michael still couldn't see him as Dina's lover, much less as her husband.

All but a few of the passengers had boarded and the passenger agent was beckoning the dawdlers. Fellows gave Dina a deep kiss, holding her in his arms with an urgency that bespoke his love. They clung to each other. Then the kiss ended, and he turned and headed for the entrance to the ramp.

"Cheerio!" Michael heard him call out. "See you in a month's time!" were his last words before he disappeared from sight.

Dina stood there for a moment, staring after him. Then she stepped to the window and peered out, though there was nothing to see but the plane. She lingered for only a minute, then returned to the concourse. She'd only gone a few steps before she saw him watching and waiting.

She had a sad expression on her face, the look of a woman who'd just said goodbye to someone she loved. He didn't like that one little bit, but he couldn't pretend he hadn't seen it. As Dina neared him, she wiped a tear from the corner of her eye. He wasn't so cynical as to believe she was acting.

"You love him, don't you?" he said as he walked beside her toward the exit.

"Yes, I do."

The sincerity in her voice weighed heavily on him. "Dina, I want you to know I respect that," he said. "Whatever else I do or say, I respect your feelings for Mason."

"Thank you. I appreciate that. And if you really mean it, the next few weeks will be more pleasant for both of us."

"It wouldn't say much for me, if I didn't put your happiness first."

"I hope those aren't just words."

"They're not."

They passed through the main lobby, and went outside toward the parking lot. The air was pungent with the smell of jet fuel and filled with the roar of aircraft engines. He turned to her.

"What is it about Mason that attracts you most? Why do you love him, if you don't mind me asking?"

A faint smile touched her lips. "Mason is eccentric, I know, but I'm attracted to that."

"Why?"

"Because he's real. He suffers, he feels, he tries, he's passionate. And he cares an awful lot about me. He wants me to succeed. We're a team. An odd couple in ways, but still a team."

Dina was saying what Mason wasn't, as much as what he was. Without saying so, she was making comparisons between him and Mason.

"I can see how that's important to you," he said. "You're deserving and he recognizes your needs."

"We clicked from the day we met."

"If you can sustain it, then I'm sure you'll be very happy together."

She glanced at him. "You aren't being sarcastic, are you, Michael?"

"No, more like wistful. I'm regretting my insights have come so late."

They came to the car and he let her in. He went around, slipping in behind the wheel. They looked at each other.

"Every experience helps a person grow," she said. "Whatever you learned from our relationship will help you do better in the next one."

He reached over and pinched her cheek. "Let's hope you're right, Dina. Let's hope you're right."

MICHAEL WAS RELATIVELY quiet during the drive to Bel Air. She hadn't anticipated his melancholy. Rather she'd expected to be treated to a dose of his characteristic charm. She wondered what, if anything, he was up to.

As they drove, she looked out at L.A. It was so different from London. Oddly, with Mason winging his way back to England, she was seeing southern California with different eyes. Over the past couple of weeks she'd been regarding it from Mason's viewpoint as much as her own. Now she was identifying more with her days as a Hollywood actress—that period of time after Michael and before Mason, when she'd tried hard to be a part of this place.

"Do you plan on staying at the Bel Air Hotel?" Michael asked. "Or do you have another place lined up?"

"Kit Mosley offered me her place in Malibu. She's leaving tomorrow to join Barry in New England where he's shooting a new picture, so I can have the house to myself and be doing her a favor at the same time."

"That's a nice break," he said. "I haven't seen Kit in forever. I'm surprised to hear she and Barry are still together. Sounds like an enduring relationship."

"They've been together six years. Says she's starting to feel like a grandmother."

"Grandmother?"

"Barry's oldest daughter had a baby recently. That may have had something to do with it."

"I imagine. He's still married, isn't he?"

"Yes. Kit says he's got the Spencer Tracy complex. She's resigned to it, though. Stopped bringing up divorce a year ago. Simply gave up on it." Dina laughed. "Since marriage is out of style anyway, she feels right in sync with the times. She won't compromise about having a baby out of wedlock, though. Says it isn't fair to the child."

"What an ancient notion," Michael said sardonically.

Dina studied him. "How is it you haven't gotten into the Hollywood swing of things, Michael? Given your success curve, you should have had three or four relationships by now and at least two children."

"I don't know. Maybe I'm a slow learner. Or a slow forgetter. I'm not sure which."

It was the closest he'd come to bringing up their past. She didn't want to get into that and opted for another tack. "I feel sorry for Kit," she said. "I think deep down she wants Barry to make it official. He won't do it, though. I guess he's got what he wants this way and sees no reason to change things."

"What would you do if Mason had a wife?"

She looked over at him, sensing a trap. "I wouldn't have let myself fall in love with him if he'd been married."

"Even if you'd been working with him . . . and had gotten to know him the way you did?"

"What is this, Michael? A morality quiz?"

"No, I'm just curious how your love for him works. Is his bachelor status part of what you love about him?"

"Of course not! You know very well what I mean when I say I wouldn't have let my feelings develop that way."

"No, I don't. Seems to me you either love a person or you don't. Their marital status may affect what action you take, but how can it affect your feelings?"

"Because love is a growing thing. It comes out of the give-and-take in a relationship. It's commitment. True, anyone can be attracted to someone who is married. But will is still part of love."

"Do you really think so?"

"Don't you?" she asked.

"I agree that people can be too emotional, act too much on instinct—"

"Or hormones."

"Yes, or hormones. But people can overthink, too. They can talk themselves into something that isn't right."

"Are you trying to say I've talked myself into loving Mason?" There was defensiveness in her voice, and it wasn't forced.

He looked surprised. "Were we talking about Mason?"

"Don't try that innocent act with me, Michael Cross. You know damned well that's what we were talking about. You brought him up."

"Maybe I wasn't as subtle as I thought. I really wasn't making a speech."

"Somehow I don't believe you."

He didn't try to defend himself. Dina was just as glad. It was becoming evident he'd opted for a quieter approach. Instead of razzle-dazzle and charm, he was going to chip away at her, plant seeds of doubt in the hope that she'd cave in and turn to him.

After a couple of minutes he said, "Mason is obviously a sensitive subject."

"You're the one who keeps bringing him up."

"Maybe we should resolve not to discuss him, then. For the sake of our work together, let's make the subject off-limits."

"Fine with me. I regard my relationship with you as essentially business anyway," she replied. "Better we keep our personal lives out of it."

"Fine. We're agreed, then. No mention of Mason from this moment on."

He'd consented to that a little too quickly. Dina wondered if she'd been had. Mason was her best defense and she'd just agreed to give him up. Well, no matter. Even if Michael had designs, he'd soon learn she meant business.

"What's next with *Cold Hearts?*" she asked. "When do I get a production schedule?"

"I was just thinking about that. We should sit down and talk. A month is a pretty narrow window to fit everything in that you'll be involved in." He stroked his chin.

"When are you going to Kit's? Tomorrow?"

"No. She's picking me up this afternoon. We're going to spend the evening together, get in the girl talk we couldn't when Mason was here—"

Michael cleared his throat.

Dina gave him a look. "I can't even make a passing reference?"

"We might as well be consistent. I won't bring him up and you won't bring him up."

"Okay. So anyway, Kit and I have a chance to talk, and that's what we plan to do."

"But she's leaving for New England tomorrow?"

"Yes, first thing in the morning. I'm driving her to the airport."

"I plan on being in Malibu myself tomorrow. I've got to get some signatures on the dotted line for the money for Ma—uh, for this film I've agreed to produce."

She laughed. "See, it isn't easy!"

He frowned. "It'll be difficult for both of us. So, getting back to tomorrow, I should be done with my meeting around eleven. How about if I drop by Kit's afterward? We can review the production schedule, discuss my plans for the film and maybe call out for a pizza."

"Wouldn't it be better if we met at your office or the studio or something?" she said, warily.

"I suggested Kit's because I'll be in the neighborhood. Why, what are you afraid of? I don't bite. Unless, of course, I've been invited to." A broad grin crept across his face.

Dina felt herself turn red. She used to love it when he nibbled at her nipples, especially when they were hard and she was fully aroused. Michael knew how to use his teeth and tongue and lips better than any man she'd known. There was a fine line between pleasure and pain, and he had it down to a tee.

They exited the freeway and came to a stop at the foot of the off-ramp. He glanced over at her.

"What's the matter? Did I say something offensive?"

"Oh, shut up, Michael!" she snapped. "Don't play dumb. You know exactly what happened. And I don't appreciate it. I think we should outlaw sexual repartee as well as references to Mason."

"But that isn't fair. It would be like cutting out my tongue!"

She couldn't help herself. She reached over and slugged him, whacking him really hard.

"Developed a taste for S&M, I see."

"I'm warning you," she said, only half as angry as she tried to sound. "This won't work if you insist on making a game of it. I want a professional relationship. Period."

"All right, Lady Winterhalter, I'll do my best."

"And cut the Lady Winterhalter bit, too."

"Dina, my love, you're trying to emasculate me. Deny me my sexuality, my wit, my fond recollections of times past. What will be left?"

She looked him dead in the eye. "Your money, Michael. Your money."

5

DINA WAS STRETCHED OUT on a lounge chair on Kit's sun porch, overlooking the beach. The glass windbreak kept off the chill of the ocean breeze, allowing her to be warmed by the sun. She had on one of Kit's straw hats and a light blue jogging suit. The script of *Cold Hearts* was lying open on her lap. She looked up from it now and then to watch the breakers rolling in and to savor the intoxicating smell of the sea.

Sid Berman had called right after she'd gotten back from dropping Kit off at LAX. "Nice work, kid," he'd said cheerfully. "You nailed the lead opposite Mike Cross and got him to finance Mason's picture. Got any other tricks up your sleeve I should know about?"

"No, that's my triumph for the year, Sid."

"Well, I got the contracts by courier this morning. Everything looks fine. I already put Mason's in an overnight to London. When and where do you want to sign yours, doll? Want me to courier it to you, or what?"

"Whatever's easiest. I can come by sometime in the next couple of days."

"Cross wants it back right away. I can come up to Malibu if you want me to go over it with you. There's nothing unusual in it, though. It's pretty straightforward."

"Does it have a clause tying *Cold Hearts* to the financing of *Green September?*"

"Yes, it's here."

Dina had been secretly hoping that there'd be a hitch, that something would go wrong, that the deal would flip and that she could get on a plane for London to be with Mason. No such luck. "Just courier it to me, Sid," she'd said. "Michael's going to drop by in a while so we can discuss the production schedule. If the contract arrives while he's here, I'll just give his copy to him."

"You got it, babe."

She'd hung up the phone. The message light was still blinking on the answering machine—she'd deliberately left it on as a reminder to call her mother back, but that was the last thing she wanted to do right now.

They had spoken twice since she'd returned to California, and Dina had avoided mentioning the possibility of doing a film with Michael both times. It had been fairly easy to rationalize the omission—talk was cheap in Hollywood and deals fell apart hourly. Now there would be no avoiding it.

She sighed. In spite of the fact that she and Michael had split up five years ago, Dina was certain that, in her heart of hearts, her mother still held out hope that they would get back together someday. And God knows, it didn't help that her mother had never warmed to Mason. Dina would never forget the way Bernice had blandly said, "To each his own, dear," when Dina had stupidly asked her mother what she thought of him.

To top it off, Bernice Winterhalter hadn't resorted to angry words or a chilly tone of voice to convey her feelings. Dina had the Oscar, but she knew she didn't have a patch on her mother when it came to acting. One look was all the woman needed to convey volumes!

Dina almost picked up the phone again, just to get it over with, then she decided to put it off until that evening. There was no need being more upset than she already was when Michael arrived, and if there was anything she could count on, it was that her mother would say something upsetting when she found out about *Cold Hearts*.

Instead, Dina picked up the script again and began reading. For nearly an hour she tried to put herself inside Alice's skin—something she could normally do with ease. But she found herself resisting. The last thing she wanted to do was identify with someone like Alice, who was still in love with her old lover—in this case Michael's character, Link.

Dina closed the script and held it to her breast like a guilt-ridden mother cuddling an unwanted child. Damn Michael to hell!

She'd dreamed about him the night before. An erotic dream. She'd had an orgasm in her sleep, awakening in a sweat, her heart pounding, mumbling his name.

She knew not to make too much of that. After all, she'd dreamed of having sex with other men many times before, even when engaged to Michael. God knows, she hadn't been sexually deprived back then. Even so, she resented it that her subconscious chose him now.

Dina looked at her watch. Michael was due at any time. She'd tried to be cavalier about it, behave the way she would if it were Barry Stewart or any other director coming to discuss a film. But, try as she might, she was edgy.

Had she overestimated her ability to keep everything in perspective? It wasn't that Michael was irresistible, because he wasn't. Still, there was no denying that she couldn't extricate him from her thoughts.

If only Michael hadn't wanted to come to the house to meet with her. A home was too intimate a setting to discuss business, and yet she had yielded. That was a mistake. She should have insisted they meet elsewhere. She'd considered dressing more formally for the meeting—to make a point—but that would have been silly. Maybe the trouble was she was making too big a deal out of it. Just because she'd once had great sex with the man didn't mean she had to be intimidated by him now.

Dina tossed the script aside and went indoors. Kit's "house" was scarcely a cottage, with one bedroom, a tiny office that Barry often used, a kitchen and bath, plus the sitting room, which overlooked the deck. Its virtue was its location. Dina figured the purchase price was the better part of a million dollars. Somehow, though, Kit's getting the house instead of a ring and a child didn't seem like that great a deal.

Kit had transported the personality of her apartment in the Hollywood Hills to Malibu. She still had her funky furniture, her paintings and objets d'art. The pictures of Barry had multiplied, however. There were half a dozen scattered around the sitting room and three more in the bedroom. Dina surmised that they were there for Barry's sake as much as for Kit's.

While the ambience was pleasant enough, Dina had a strong sense of the illicitness of the place. It was Barry Stewart's mistress's hideaway. Their love nest. Not that Dina was a prude—she shared Mason's place with him in London, though she had a flat of her own to escape to when she needed space. But Mason was single, and they *did* plan to marry

Dina stared at herself in the antique-framed mirror in the sitting room. She smoothed her hair, wondering at her unhappy state of mind. Then she plopped down in the big wicker armchair that dominated the room. She closed her eyes and listened to the muted pounding of the surf.

Feeling more peaceful than she'd been all morning, Dina was startled by the sudden sound of knocking. She went to the front door and opened it. Michael was standing there, wearing jeans and a red cashmere sweater. His eyes were masked by sunglasses, his hair slightly mussed by the wind. He had a stylishly worn leather briefcase in his hand and that familiar grin on his face.

"How's my leading lady?" he asked.

Behind him, only yards away, the traffic was whizzing by on the Coast Highway. The sun reflected off the windshield of his Jaguar, making her squint to see him clearly.

"Your leading lady has been dutifully studying the script." She stepped back to admit him.

"How's it holding up?" he asked, as she closed the door.

"I like it. I just hope I'll be able to do Alice justice."

He gave her an inquisitive look. "Is there something about her that bothers you?"

"It's not the writing. She's well drawn and motivated."

"But?"

"Let's go sit down."

Dina led the way to the sitting room. She gestured for him to take the wicker chair, but he headed straight for the wall of glass instead, setting down his briefcase and looking out at the beach. After a moment he turned around. "So, what's the problem?"

Dina had sat down in a leather wing chair that looked more like it belonged in a formal library than a Malibu beach house. She assumed it was Barry's contribution. "I don't want to sound like a spoiled starlet."

"If you're having misgivings, I should know. Talk to me about it."

"It isn't the script, Michael. It's me."

"What's wrong with you?"

"I don't know if I can do Alice."

"Why not?"

"I'm not *feeling* her." She shook her head. "And that's not like me. I've never had this happen before. Roles usually never give me problems, but this one is."

"Would you like Dr. Cross to help you analyze it?"

"I'd like for Dr. Cross to accept the fact that it isn't a good fit. Perhaps Producer-Director Cross would be better off finding another actress."

Michael went over and sat in the wicker chair. He crossed his legs and regarded her. "I want you to play Alice."

"Yes, I know. I'm not trying to give you a hard time. I feel terrible about this. And it's not at all professional."

"It isn't me, by any chance, is it?"

She drew a long breath, seeing no point in fighting it any longer. "You know it is."

"You can't bear the thought of getting into bed with me, even under the lights with a dozen people looking on?"

"It's stupid, I know," she said, lowering her eyes. "And I *can* go through the motions, if you absolutely insist. But that's not fair to you. If an actor's not feeling a role, it can only lead to disaster. You know that as well as I do."

"Once you're on the set everything will fall into place."

"But what if it doesn't?"

"Then we'll make a bad picture."

"I don't want that to happen, for either of our sakes."

"I'm willing to take the chance because I'm sure we can make it work. I'll need your cooperation, though."

She gave him a woebegone look.

"We've acted together often enough that the ground will feel familiar in no time. I promise you."

She shook her head. "That was ages ago. You're making assumptions about the way things are now."

He gave her one of his charming smiles. "Want to bet?"

"What kind of bet? My fee, double or nothing?"

"Oh, come on," he chided. "Let me prove that you can do Alice." He glanced around. "Where's the script?"

"Oh, I believe I left it out on the deck."

Michael got up and went outside. He returned with a bemused expression on his face. Holding up the script, he pointed to a big white splotch on the cover. "We've been visited by angels."

"Angels?"

"Well, maybe a sea gull."

Dina couldn't help laughing. "It's an omen, Michael."

"The bird of paradise," he said.

"No, I was thinking something else."

He went into the kitchen and returned a moment later, having wiped off the cover. He handed her the script, then sat down on the ottoman that matched the wing chair. He told her to turn to the final scene between Alice and Link. The setting was the Crown Room, a bar at the top of the Fairmont Hotel in San Francisco. They were seated by the window, looking out at the bay and the twinkling lights of the city. The bad guys had been caught or killed, the undercover operation was over. All that remained was for Alice and Link to have their last farewell.

Dina looked at him, waiting.

"Let's do the scene," he said.

"Now?"

"Yes, now."

"Won't you have to look at the script?"

"I know the lines enough to get by."

She took a deep breath. Michael was daring her to fail, challenging her pride. This was the most emotionally dramatic scene in the film and they both knew it.

"Go ahead," he said.

Dina closed her eyes for a second to gather herself. Then she began. "'Why did you bring me here, Link?'" she read. "'It's the cruelest thing you've ever done.'"

"'I had to. There was no other choice.'"

"'Why?'" she said, her voice trembling. "'Because you had to see me cry?'"

Dina could hear the hollowness in her voice. She wasn't convincing herself, so she knew darn well she wasn't convincing Michael.

"'I had to bring you back where it all began,'" he said. "'For this one last time.'"

"'Still, it's selfish. And I don't want to think of you as selfish. Ever. It will only ruin what we've shared.'"

Michael reached over and took her hand. Dina felt herself stiffen.

"'How can being with the woman I love be selfish?'" he asked. "'I'd give my life for you, Alice. You know that.'"

As he said his lines, Michael rubbed the backs of her fingers with his thumb, sending tremors up and down her spine. She had to struggle not to react, to stay in character.

"'If you loved me, you'd take pity on me,'" she said. "'You wouldn't put me through this. The decent thing would be to go, to get up and walk from the room without looking back.'"

Michael pulled her hand to his mouth. He kissed her knuckles, blowing his warm breath on them. Then he rubbed her hand against his cheek. "'Just a few more minutes,'" he murmured. "'Give me that. I want to burn your image into my brain.'"

Tears welled in her eyes. "'Oh, please don't do this to me, Link. Please. Go. Please, go.'"

A tear rolled over her lid and down her cheek. Michael touched it with his fingertip. Then kissed it. "'I'll never forget you,'" he whispered. "'Never.'"

The script began shaking in her hand. Dina looked at him through bleary eyes. She was crying now, virtually on the point of sobbing. The screenplay didn't call for her to embrace him then, but she wanted to. She wanted to put her arms around his neck and weep.

There was a loud knock, startling her. Dina gave a little cry before catching herself. She looked into Mi-

chael's eyes. They were teary, too. She drew a ragged
breath.

"Someone's at the door," she murmured.

"Yes, I think you're right." He still held her hand and
only then did Dina realize she was squeezing his fingers.
"I'll get it," he said. Michael stood, but he didn't walk
away. Instead he leaned over and lightly kissed her. "You
make a wonderful Alice." Without waiting for a reply,
he went off to get the door.

Dina fell back in the chair, her insides mush. She wiped
her cheeks with the backs of her hands. How did he know
that would happen? she wondered. It was scary to think
she was so malleable—that he could arouse her emotions so easily. Michael had been right. It had happened
countless times before, when they were together on the
stage. But this had been different.

She could hear voices without distinctly making out
what was being said. Then she heard the door close. Michael returned to the sitting room. He had a manila envelope in his hand.

"Courier for you," he said.

For a second her brain was too muddled to figure out
what could be in the envelope. Then she remembered Sid
was sending over the contracts. Michael handed it to her.

"They're my contracts," she said. "My agent sent them
to me. I'm supposed to sign them, but I'm not so sure I
should."

Michael sat on the ottoman. He took both her hands
in his. "Once you got warmed up, you were great, Dina.
I only wish I had a camera and crew here."

"Quit trying to flatter me, Michael. I was terrible."

"You made *me* cry, and I wrote the stuff."

"You were projecting," she said. "It had nothing to do with my acting."

The corners of his mouth lifted. "I have a hunch that if you and I do a good job of 'projecting' on each other, the audience will be satisfied."

He kissed both her hands. Dina flashed on the night he'd proposed. For a brief intense moment, Malibu became Seattle and she loved him again, loved him with heart-wrenching intensity.

"You're a devil, Michael Cross," she said softly, as she signed the contracts and gave Michael his copy. He asked if she wanted him to have a pizza delivered, but she said she wasn't hungry. Instead she fixed them both some coffee and the two of them sat at the tiny kitchen table and ran through the production schedule.

"I'd like to do three days of interiors here in L.A. at the studio," he said. "Then a couple of weeks of location shooting in San Francisco. Because I've only got a month, I'm going to keep you hopping."

"I prefer working quickly. Anyway, I'm eager to get back to London."

Michael let that pass without comment. "I've done several of my scenes already and I'll finish up after you go. Most of our work will be in San Francisco."

"I like it up there."

"Yes, I do, too. It's a lot like Seattle. And vice versa."

Seattle, she could see, had become a code word for their past. In an odd way, *Cold Hearts* itself was a parody of their life together; she'd noticed that with her first reading of the screenplay. And the implied message had not been lost on her. That was probably part of the reason she'd resisted taking the role.

After they'd finished their coffee and gone over the schedule in detail, Michael said he had to go. She'd been only minimally hospitable, doing her best to keep things businesslike. She was relieved when he didn't try to turn it into a social occasion.

When he'd packed up his briefcase, Dina went with him to the door. He reached out and caressed her face, more in a friendly way than a sexual one.

"I don't want you worrying about anything," he said. "Doing this picture right is a top priority. Whatever I can do to help you, I will."

"Give me lots of space off the set, Michael. That's more important than anything."

"I promised that nothing would happen you didn't want to happen," he said, "and I meant it."

"Thank you."

Michael leaned over, gave her a peck on the cheek, then went out into the sunshine. After closing the door Dina returned to the deck, where she sat for an hour watching the breakers rolling in, and thinking about Seattle.

6

DINA FINISHED IN MAKEUP and walked across the lot in a heavy white terry robe and slip-ons. The wind was brisk, nipping at her bare ankles and face. Under the robe she had on a bikini bottom—and that was it. She was scheduled to shoot a shower scene in which there would be a profile shot of her breasts. She had been nervous about it all morning and it had shown in her work. They had done one scene five times before Michael was satisfied.

Afterward he'd put his arm around her shoulders. "If I'd known you were going to be so uptight about taking a shower for me, I'd have taken the crew to Malibu this morning and shot you in your own bathroom, at home," he teased. "It would have saved me a reel of film."

"I'm sorry, Michael," she'd said. "For some reason, being naked bothers me. I've never taken a shower for the camera before."

Of course, it wasn't the camera so much as it was him. She knew what he'd be thinking as he watched her. The love scenes, which he planned to do on location in San Francisco, would be even worse.

The first two days of shooting had gone smoothly. She had acted with Michael in a couple of brief scenes but most of her work had been with other actors, or alone. As a director Michael had been patient, supportive and very professional. She couldn't be around him without feeling the sexual awareness, of course, but he'd done nothing overt to make her uncomfortable. Actually, just the opposite. But the shower scene would be a major test of her feelings . . . and her ability to deal with them.

She entered the studio where the assistant director, Natalie Harris, was waiting for her. Natalie was a brunette with owlish glasses. She was three years out of film school and dying to do her own film. Natalie was nice, if a little overly solicitous. As a rule actors weren't indulged as much in England, so Dina had to get used to the pampering all over again.

"I know it's cool in here," Natalie said, "but we've got space heaters on the set so you won't be too uncomfortable."

"Just so the water's hot. I hate a cold shower."

"It'll be warm. That's the most I can promise. If it's too hot we have problems with steam. The technical people have been working on it."

Dina rolled her eyes. "I'm only going to do films with bathtub scenes from now on."

Natalie laughed dutifully. They got to the set, where Michael was busy with the technicians and the stage crew.

"We're here," Natalie announced.

Michael turned and acknowledged them with a nod. "I'll be right there," he said, his eyes briefly gliding down her.

Dina clasped the lapels of the robe at her throat and stood watching. After a minute Michael came over, clipboard in hand. He was in a black turtleneck sweater and charcoal cords. His sunglasses were pushed up into his hair.

"Have a good lunch?" he asked cordially.

"Yes, it was fine, thanks," she said.

The first day at the studio he'd invited her to lunch, but she'd told him she preferred a quick sandwich in her dressing room because she wanted to telephone London. "It's a good time there to reach a director friend of mine," she'd explained, faithful to her promise not to mention Mason by name. Michael had taken the hint and backed off. He didn't invite her to eat with him the next two days in deference to her evident wishes.

"I've got this scene blocked," he said. "Let me run through it with you." Using the clipboard, he showed her what he wanted, noting the camera angles. "Remember, you're thinking about your previous night with Link. The sex was great. You feel fabulous. I want to see the recollection of the physical passion on your face in the close-ups."

"I presume it's all right if I inspire myself with a mental image of someone else."

The corners of Michael's mouth curled. "Sure, if you can do better than Link, be my guest."

"You want me convincing, don't you?"

"Where you get your great sex is your business, Dina."

She smiled. "Thank you."

"I've been thinking about the best way to get the effect I want," he said, returning to the matter at hand. "I'd like a full-length shot of you completely naked, stepping into the shower. It'll be a three-quarters angle from behind. They may make me cut it, but I want to try to get it past the censors if I can. I hate being coy."

"You're saying you want me prancing around naked before the camera, so you can experiment."

"The more footage I have to work with, the better. And yes, I'll be doing some improvising. But I promise I'll be reasonable."

Dina didn't like the notion of cavorting around nude any more than she had to. "Just don't put me through an ordeal, Michael. I feel uncomfortable enough already about this."

"You occupy your mind with the fantasy of your choice and let me worry about the rest."

She gave him a look. "You're making this sound like a seduction."

He grinned. "You think so?"

"And I don't mean that as a compliment." Dina glanced around the set at the waiting crew. "Can we do the skin stuff first and get it over with?"

"Certainly."

Michael turned to Alex Kempel, the rumpled little gray-haired director of photography, and talked about the sequence of shots. The gaffer joined them to discuss changes in lighting. Natalie had one of the grips bring Dina a chair and move a space heater closer.

Dina closed her eyes to get herself into her character. She mentally ran through the action, tuning herself to Alice's emotion, sensuality and feeling of sexual satisfaction. Dina intended to use her lovemaking with Mason to inspire herself, but the partner who came to mind was Michael. It had been five long years, but she had a clear recollection of the way it had been with him, the feel of his tongue on her skin—the way he'd lick the undersides of her breasts, her neck, the insides of her thighs.

Opening her eyes, she looked over at him, hoping that would help jar her back into reality. It didn't. His back was to her. She stared at his derriere, his legs. Despite herself, she fell right back into the fantasy. She envisioned him naked. She recalled the feel of his skin when they made love, the desire she always had to claw at him with her nails, the spent feeling after her orgasm, the rubbery sensation in her muscles when she climbed from bed or into the shower afterward.

This was exactly what Michael had in mind. This was the way he wanted her thinking. He wanted her to remember—not so much for the sake of his movie, perhaps, as for himself.

He finished his conversation and came over to her. "So, how do you feel?"

What did he expect her to say? Aroused? "I feel okay, but I do want this over with."

He put his hand on her shoulder and began kneading the muscles. "Hey, you're all knotted up." He moved around behind her and began massaging her shoulders with his thumbs. "We've got to get you loose and relaxed."

It felt so good that Dina didn't object. He was right; she had to relax and get her body supple. She had to think sensual, she had to get into Alice's head. Dina closed her eyes and tried to go with the sensation, put out of her mind who was massaging her body.

"I should have gotten a masseuse in here to get you loosened up. I wasn't thinking."

"I'll be all right," she said, starting to feel really good.

"Natalie!" he called to his assistant.

Dina heard the woman promptly arriving at Michael's side. "Yes?"

"Let's get a masseuse in for Dina whenever we're doing something sensual—the love scenes, whatever."

"All right, I'll make a note. I can have somebody here every morning, if you want."

"Would you like that, Dina?" he asked, leaning over her. He was still massaging her. It was heaven.

"No, it's not necessary. I'm not always this tense."

"It's one of the fringe benefits of being my leading lady," he said. Then to Natalie, he said, "Get her a masseuse."

"Check." Natalie went away.

Dina turned and looked up at him. "Are you trying to spoil me?"

"You mean to say living in England you aren't used to getting the royal treatment?"

It was a thinly veiled dig, aimed at Mason, which she didn't much appreciate. "Not while I'm working," she replied. "And we don't talk about when I'm not working. The subject's off-limits."

"Yeah, right," he said.

She took a deep breath. "I'm ready, Michael."

"Okay, let's run through it a couple of times with your robe on." He turned to the crew. "Give me some quiet, please. We're going to go through this."

A hush fell over the studio as Dina got to her feet. Michael went with her to the enclosed shower stall. Adjacent to it was a two-sided mock-up stall they'd be using for the close-up shots inside the stall and under the shower head.

Referring to his clipboard, Michael demonstrated what he wanted her to do. She would reach in to turn on the water, though the flow was actually controlled by a technician offstage. Then, her back to the camera, she'd remove her robe and toss it on a stool before stepping into the stall.

"The trick will be making it look natural," he said. "The camera will be observing an intimate moment, not a striptease."

"Thank God for small favors."

"The scene will stand or fall by the shots close on your face, Dina. That's where the sensuality will be conveyed. But we've got to see your body, however briefly, to put it in a context."

"Okay, Michael. Let's do it."

He reached out, slipping his hand behind her neck. He massaged the cords of her neck. "Want to rehearse it once, exactly as you'll do it?"

"No, let's shoot it. I might get lucky and do it right the first time."

"Fine. There's something to be said for spontaneity," he said, giving her a wink. "All right, everybody," he said, turning to the crew, "let's do a take. Alex." Michael retreated to his place behind the camera. "Dina, position, please."

She went to her mark. She took a couple of moments to become Alice. When she nodded that she was ready, Michael called for action.

Dina reached into the shower. The water came on. She withdrew her arm from the stall, loosened the tie of her robe and let it drop.

"Cut!" Michael called out. "Dina, darling . . ."

There were a few snickers, then she realized what was wrong. She had on her bikini bottom. Covering her breast with an arm, she bent down and picked up the robe and slipped it back on, keeping her back to the camera and crew. She turned to face him.

"Sorry."

"Alice is not quite that shy."

"I forgot I had it on," she said, embarrassed. "I hadn't planned on a full-length shot."

"That's all right. Take it off, please, and we'll try again. I like the way you did the robe, by the way."

Dina turned around, reached under her robe and slipped her suit off. A wardrobe assistant took it from her.

"Places," Michael called out.

Dina went to her mark again. Once more she closed her eyes to get into character. She felt more vulnerable this time. It wasn't the presence of the crew that bothered her—there was a certain amount of exhibitionist in practically every actor. In a way it was easier to reveal your body under bright lights than it was to reveal your soul. But Michael's presence made it terribly difficult. He knew her body as intimately as anyone, but the fact that they were now estranged—and knowing that he wanted her—made it almost impossible. She was no longer his.

"Ready, Dina?"

"Give me a few more seconds, please."

Her head bowed, she envisioned "Link" making love to her. She felt his teeth and fingertips on her skin. She felt him, erect and hard. She felt herself moisten. She felt him drive into her. She felt climax and release. She took a couple of long, deep breaths to steady herself as little tremors went through her body. Then she nodded. "Okay, Michael," she said, her voice barely above a whisper, "I'm ready."

DINA ONLY HAD TO DO the full body shot, stepping into the shower, twice. But they worked on the close-up shots of her face for over half an hour. Michael had her move her hands sensually over her breasts, telling her he wanted her face to reflect every erotic sensation. When it was over, he told her she was magnificent. Dina was emotionally exhausted.

After wrapping herself in the terry robe, she dropped into the chair and the hairdresser toweled her hair. Michael stood facing her, his face full of admiration.

"That was great stuff, Dina. Truly. You got just the effect I wanted. I'm really pleased."

"Thank you."

"You're welcome to watch the dailies with me, if you're curious."

"Thanks, but I'd rather wait until the final cut. I work better when I'm guided by what I feel, rather than what I see."

"I guess I'll have to enjoy them alone, then. Would you mind if the outtakes wind up in my personal library?"

"Yes, I would, as a matter of fact."

"But I paid for them, didn't I?" He was teasing her.

"Well, do what you want with them. Just don't put them in a stag film."

"I wouldn't share them with my best friend."

The hairdresser had finished toweling Dina's hair dry and made a turban with a towel to keep her head warm. Dina got up from her chair.

"You're through for the day, my dear," Michael said, as they walked toward the exit, "but I've got some stunt scenes to shoot in half an hour. Would you care to join me and watch yourself hurling through the air?"

"I think not, Michael. I'm tired and I just want to go home and kick back a little."

"Let me walk you to your dressing room, then," he said. "I want to discuss a change in plans."

Dina gave him a wary look. She was always on her guard around him, knowing that at any time he could do something or say something that crossed the line. Michael had power over her and her only defense against him was to be resolute. "What sort of change?"

They exited the studio, going out into the bright sunlight. The wind had died down and it was more seasonably warm. They started across the lot.

"We've had some problems with the location arrangements in San Francisco, and I've decided to move everything to Seattle. I originally flirted with the idea of shooting the picture up there anyway, but thought you might object, so I opted for San Francisco. Now my hand's been forced, so I've had a man up in Seattle seeing if we could make the switch on a last-minute basis."

Dina wasn't quite sure what to think. "I see."

"I would have preferred to follow the original plan, but it would have been extremely difficult and probably would have required more time. This way, I can stay within budget and not lose anything. In fact, Seattle might set a more appropriate mood for the picture."

Dina walked along, listening. Michael was doing a selling job on her and she knew exactly what he was afraid she might be thinking—that if he got her back to their old stomping ground, recollections of times past might be stronger, and she might be affected. He could be right about that, and the mere possibility would be reason enough to resist. But as a practical matter, there wasn't a lot she could do about it. At least he had the decency to talk to her about it.

"Obviously Seattle has personal memories for us," she said, "but I can hardly let a thing like that bother me. I am who I am, whether I'm in London, L.A. or Seattle. I guess we'll just have to deal with it."

He grinned. "I knew you'd understand."

"You didn't think I might throw a temper tantrum over it, I hope."

"Well, maybe the past has a tighter grip on me than it does on you, Dina. Every time I'm in Seattle, you're with me in spirit. The associations are very strong for me."

"What is this," she quipped, "a negative sell?"

"No, I just want all the cards on the table. I owe you honesty if nothing else."

"You aren't telling me to expect you to misbehave, are you?"

He shook his head. "If I sin, it will only be in my imagination. You've shown you can deal with that."

They came to her dressing room. Dina stopped to face him. "Thanks for your openness, Michael. I assume it's intended as a sign of respect. But don't worry about me. I'm a professional. If you treat me like one, we won't have any problems."

Michael smiled, looking into her eyes. There was something in his expression, a seductiveness that he couldn't repress if his life depended on it. She'd come to accept that about him. But she hadn't been able to fully ignore it. Michael Cross still had a powerful effect on her. Fortunately it was only short-term. Her heart was in London with Mason.

"We leave day after tomorrow," Michael said. "Natalie will fill you in on particulars and answer any questions."

"All right. Thanks."

Michael turned and went off then. Dina stepped into her dressing room, removing the towel from her head. She went to the mirror. For some reason, she felt guilty as she looked into her eyes. Michael didn't know it, but she'd made love with him that morning. It had been the best way she knew to give him the sensuality he wanted.

7

TO DINA'S ASTONISHMENT, they arrived in Seattle on a gloriously sunny day. Most of her recollections were of slate gray skies and drizzling rain. This sparkling city was not the Seattle she'd known with Michael.

Even though there'd been a lot of rain, she hadn't minded the climate of the Pacific Northwest. There were similarities to London. Sunshine and warmth were important to her, but she could wait to get them on trips and vacations—so long as the breaks weren't too infrequent.

After they'd checked in to their hotel, a skyscraper in the downtown area affording an unobstructed view of Puget Sound, Dina stood at the big window of her suite, contemplating the panorama. During their Seattle days, she and Michael had danced at a disco located on the top floor of one of the big hotels. She couldn't remember now which one it was—she didn't even know whether it was still there—but her recollections of them standing arm in arm, looking out at the lights of the city, were still quite vivid. She wondered if Michael would substitute that setting for the farewell scene that had been slated for the Crown Room at the Fairmont in San Francisco.

Dina sighed. It was stupid to indulge herself in nostalgia. Michael, damn him, would do a good enough job of that without her help. What she needed was to get her mind off the past. A call to Mason would help, but it was too late. In London it was already approaching midnight.

While they were riding in from the airport Michael had told her he had lots to do that afternoon, though they wouldn't start shooting until the next day. That meant she was free to rest or wander around and reacquaint herself with Seattle, if she chose. But he'd insisted he wanted to take her to dinner, saying he had a surprise for her.

Dina had been reluctant to accept. She didn't want to commit herself without giving it some thought. Michael had been on relatively good behavior, so she had no grounds for complaint. Obviously, at some point her unyielding attitude would start to look childish and defensive, if it hadn't already. And yet her instincts told her Michael was a danger to her. Humoring him could prove to be a fatal mistake.

On the other hand, she couldn't hide from her feelings forever. Just being in Seattle had made her feel nostalgic. Michael had probably been counting on that, as well, but that didn't make it any less true. After all, until Mason had come along, Michael had been the love of her life. They had shared some wonderful times. The difference between them was that she understood there was no going back. But did that mean she could safely reminisce a little, for old times' sake?

After her luggage was delivered, Dina had room service bring her some tea. She tried to relax, leafing through the script and thinking about Michael's proposal. It was probably silly to make such a big deal out of a dinner invitation, but deep down she was certain that more than dinner was at stake. The telephone rang just then. It was Michael.

"Have you decided about tonight?" he asked.

She hadn't. She was still vacillating. "We're just talking dinner, right?"

"Just dinner."

Dina was really fighting herself and she didn't like that at all. But her dignity and her pride were as much at stake as her well-being. Deciding to throw caution to the winds, she accepted.

"Great," he said. "I'll be tied up for three or four hours. How about if I meet you in the lobby at six o'clock?"

"Okay, fine."

"See you then."

Dina hung up, certain she'd made the wrong decision. But she told herself that whether she went or not wasn't nearly as important as how she handled it once they were together.

When she'd finished her tea, she grabbed her coat and sunglasses and went downstairs. The doorman got her a taxi, which she took to Pioneer Square. If she wanted to indulge in some nostalgia, better she do it in the shops.

Unlike Michael, who'd been mobbed by fans at the airport, asking for autographs and trying to touch him, Dina was rarely approached in public. With sunglasses on she could move about almost unrecognized, though from time to time people would give her inquiring looks, as though she seemed familiar. The exposure she'd get for *Cold Hearts* would probably change that some, which was why Sid Berman had been eager for her to take on the project. The lead in one big hit could make her instantly recognizable.

Dina managed to browse in half a dozen shops before a clerk in a lingerie boutique recognized her. "Aren't you Dina Winters, the movie star?" the girl asked tentatively.

"Yes," Dina said, amused and flattered as she always was when someone found the courage to ask. "You saw through my disguise."

"My boyfriend loved *Revenge of the Ghouls.*"

"I'm glad somebody did," she said.

"He'll die when I tell him I saw you. Can I have your autograph? He'll never believe me unless I can prove I actually talked to you."

"Sure."

The clerk produced a scrap of paper and asked her to sign it "For Donny." Two other customers came over to see what was going on. When they discovered who Dina was, they became excited, too. One, a chunky little blonde, enthusiastically told Dina she'd seen *Mirabella* three times and loved the film.

"I wish there'd been a few million more people like you."

They all laughed.

"Are you making a movie in Seattle?" the third woman asked.

Dina explained what she was doing in town. At the mention of Michael's name, the little blonde went into giddy hysterics.

"He is *so* good-looking and sexy," she gushed. "How can you stand next to him without your knees buckling?"

"You get used to it, like anything else," Dina said with a smile.

"If Michael Cross kissed me, I'd just die," the woman said.

The others nodded their agreement.

"Is he anything like he is in his movies?" she asked.

"No, that's not Michael at all," Dina replied.

"What's he really like?"

"Michael's intelligent, serious, sensitive, down-to-earth. Not at all spoiled by success." There was a tremor in her voice. The women seemed to notice. "He's a friend," she added. "We've known each other a long time."

There was a silence and Dina realized she'd been defending Michael and wondered why. Perhaps what she was defending was the past.

Dina signed autographs for the other two women before she left, saying goodbye to her new fans. She walked briskly up the street, escaping, though it wasn't clear from what. Then she understood what had happened. She'd talked about Michael the way she normally would about Mason. She wondered if that was a bad sign. Over the last several days, the tension between her and Michael had been melting away. She was starting to let down her guard—the one thing she'd told herself she couldn't do.

Feeling a kind of confused desperation, Dina turned her thoughts to Mason. *He* was her salvation. Now, more than ever, he was important to her well-being, if not her sanity. If she could keep her mind on him, she'd be all right. *Mason, Mason, Mason,* she said to herself, using his name over and over again like a mantra. *Don't forsake me. I need you.*

DINA ENTERED THE HOTEL with barely enough time to get cleaned up and changed before meeting Michael. She'd gone from wariness to downright fear. The surprise he'd talked about had her wondering. She couldn't imagine what it could be, and was afraid to find out.

A bellhop carried her packages up to her suite. She told him to dump everything on the sofa in the sitting room, gave him a couple of dollars and then he left. Her main purchase had been an antique Regulator clock for Mason, which she'd had shipped to London. She'd also bought him a tie, but she would take that with her. The other purchases were odds and ends she'd gotten for herself, and a nice crystal bowl for Kit.

Then Dina went into the bathroom for a quick shower. She'd just finished dressing and doing her hair when the telephone rang. It was Mason.

"Darling," she said, surprised, "what are you doing up? Isn't it the middle of the night there?"

"I couldn't sleep. I decided I needed to hear your voice."

"That's sweet, darling. I miss you, too." Dina was glad. She needed a connection with him. She needed a buffer against Michael.

"Do you really?" he asked.

"Of course. Why do you sound surprised?"

"I don't know," he said. "I guess I'm in a black mood. What are you doing now?"

Was there suspicion in his voice, or was she imagining it? Suddenly she felt traitorous. "Just getting ready to go out for a bite. It's dinnertime."

Dina knew she was making it sound like she was going to run down to the coffee shop when in fact she was going out with Michael. Dammit, she hated herself for doing that.

"So how's everything?" he asked. "Is *Cold Hearts* going to be a hit?"

Dina was glad for an excuse to talk shop. They chatted about Michael's film and she asked Mason about preparations for *Green September*. He gave her a detailed rundown. When they ran out of things to say, there were mutual expressions of love, then they said goodbye.

Dina sat on the bed afterward. She felt dreadful. Was it too late to cancel dinner with Michael, or would that be even dumber than accepting the invitation in the first place? She looked at the clock. She was already late. Gathering her purse and coat, she went downstairs. Michael was waiting in the lobby.

"Sorry to be late," she said. "I was on a transatlantic call."

The briefest look of displeasure crossed his face, and was quickly replaced by a smile. "No problem, I was a few minutes late myself."

Michael took her arm and, with people looking at them, they went out of the hotel to a limousine waiting at the curb. Dina climbed in first and Michael followed, sitting close beside her.

"So," she said, noticing he had on that cologne again, the one he'd worn years earlier, "what's the surprise?"

"There are two surprises, actually, but I can't tell you what they are. I have to show you."

His response gave her pause, but she saw no point in pressing him. Whatever Michael had up his sleeve, she'd deal with it. She'd left herself without much choice.

They drove down toward the waterfront, much of which had been redeveloped and upgraded over the past several years. It was familiar territory. Her loft had been in that general area and so had their theater. When they headed up the street where their theater had been, she began wondering what Michael was up to. Sure enough, they stopped in front of it.

"Why have we come here?" she asked.

Michael looked at her proudly. "It's mine again," he replied.

"What?"

"I bought it back." Then he tossed his head. "Come on, let's have a look."

They got out of the limo and went to the door. Michael unlocked it. Once inside, he turned on the lights. There was scaffolding around and construction materials. It was apparent the place was being refurbished.

"I'm completely redoing it," he explained. "I've upgraded the stage and we'll be putting in new seats and increasing the capacity to three hundred."

"Michael, what for? Why are you doing this?"

He surveyed the dimly lit stage from where they stood at the back of the theater. "I suppose the honest answer is because I miss it. I've bought a house up here and plan to split my time between Seattle and L.A. During the hiatus between pictures I'm going to put on plays. I'll produce, direct a few and maybe even act in one now and again."

Dina heard the nostalgia in his voice. Stage actors, regardless of whatever other successes they enjoyed, never lost their love for the theater. She understood that. She felt much the same way.

"Come on," he said, taking her hand. "Let's go on-stage." Michael led the way down one of the side aisles and they climbed up on the stage.

Dina surveyed the dark theater.

"So, what do you think?" he asked.

"I think maybe you're having an identity crisis, Michael," she said with a laugh, then walked across the stage, to get a feel for it. She had always liked the theater and Michael's little charade had served to remind her of that, if nothing else. But she didn't want to wallow in sentiment too long. She knew it could be dangerous.

She glanced back at him. His eyes were on her. Admiringly.

"I'd like to do a play with you again sometime," he said. "I always thought we worked well together on the stage."

"Unless you intend to be in London, that might be difficult," she replied.

She watched his expression to see how he took her rebuff. When his mouth widened to a bemused grin, she was relieved. "It's time for your second surprise," he said.

They left the stage. Dina started feeling guilty as they made their way toward the exit. Maybe she'd been a little hard on him. Her crack about an identity crisis had been unkind.

"I like what you're doing here, Michael," she said in a conciliatory tone. "I'm sure you'll get a lot of enjoyment from it."

"I hope so."

They got back into the limousine. Dina found herself in a reflective mood. She turned her mind to what was next. Michael had mentioned another surprise. She wondered what in the world it could be.

They'd driven for only a few blocks before she began to suspect they were heading for her old apartment. "You aren't taking me on another trip down memory lane, are you?"

"Sort of," he confessed. "But I think you'll like it."

Moments later they pulled up in front of her old apartment building. Dina sat staring at the entrance, then she turned to him. "Michael, why are you doing this?"

"Try just going with it. It'll be fine. Come on."

He got out of the limo. Dina hesitated a long moment before following him. Michael helped her out, taking her hand and holding it as they walked to the entry. He took a key from his pocket and let them in.

"You have a key?"

"Yes. I own the place. Bought it a couple of months ago."

First the theater and now her building. It was a trend that was getting more disturbing. "Why?"

"Call me sentimental."

"Why are we going inside?"

"I thought you'd like to see your old apartment."

"Don't tell me you kicked somebody out just so you could show it to me."

"The tenant was a nice young lady who was more than happy to accept a generous lease-termination settlement from me. I think she bought herself a new car with the money I gave her."

"Michael . . ."

"Nobody got hurt, Dina. Everybody's happy."

She was annoyed by his presumption. What made him think he could do this? And what did he hope to achieve?

They took the elevator to the top floor—her floor. Michael led the way to her door. He started to open it. She took his arm. "What are you expecting, Michael? That I'm going to get all sentimental and succumb?"

"That's a rather cynical way to put it, isn't it?"

"No," she said, shaking her head. "You bringing me here is thoughtless. And selfish. The theater was okay, but this is going too far."

His expression turned sober. "I certainly don't mean it selfishly."

"You couldn't have thought I wanted this."

"I know the days we spent here together are over. I know you're convinced that how we felt about each other is over, too. I guess I'm not as sure about that as you are, and so I'm going with what I feel."

"Michael, it *is* over!" she said adamantly.

"I haven't even opened the door."

Dina shook her head. "Don't do this, please. You promised me."

"I promised you that you wouldn't have to do anything you didn't want to do. But if you're right that the past is dead, then you have nothing to fear."

"That's cheap rhetoric. You know damned well this isn't fair."

"What are you afraid of? Just tell me."

"Michael, stop it. I want to go." She started to turn away, but he took her arm.

"Just have a look," he said, almost pleading with her. "I went to a lot of trouble to arrange this. I even tried to match your furniture as well as I could remember it. What's wrong with taking a peek?"

Dina gave him a long hard look, then sighed. "All right, but I'm only going to glance around."

Michael let her into the apartment. She was greeted with the warm glow of a crackling fire. And there was her white sofa, or one very like it. She looked around, amazed. The pictures were different, but they were similar in mood. He'd done a masterful job. It was like going back in time to the rainy evenings they'd spent together in front of the fire with glasses of wine, talking, dreaming, making love.

Her eyes filled with tears. For the first time, she had a strong emotional reaction to memories of their days together. She'd already grieved the loss of that love. She'd put it behind her. Until a few weeks ago Michael Cross had been exorcised from her life. But he was with her now and they were together in a place where they had been so deeply in love. Being in her loft, seeing it, smelling it, made her remember everything—oh, so vividly.

Michael was watching her. She avoided looking at him for as long as she could, glancing around the room with bleary eyes. There was a vase of yellow roses on the table, books on the bookshelf.

"I can see you went to a lot of trouble," she murmured. "But I wish you hadn't."

"It doesn't hurt, does it?"

She turned to him then. He was leaning against the door, his trench coat hanging from his clasped hands, and looking sad as the light from the fire played on his face. He'd seemed so self-confident since their reunion that it startled her to see a touch of uncertainty in him now.

"It does hurt, Michael. It's like seeing a picture of a dead friend, someone you'd once been close to. Yes, it hurts."

"That's not what I intended."

"I know."

"It doesn't bring you even a little joy?"

She shook her head. "I wish it did, but it doesn't."

"Then I guess I have to ask your forgiveness."

"That's not necessary," she said. "But I would like to go."

"All right. A catered dinner is going to be delivered here shortly, but we can scrap that and go to that fish place up the street we both liked. Or someplace else, if you prefer."

"Would you hate me if I asked you to take me back to the hotel? I'd just as soon skip eating."

"You're that upset?"

"Yes, but I don't blame you. I know you meant well. I just don't want to go back, like you do."

He looked into her shimmering eyes. "I'm sorry, Dina," he said, his voice cracking slightly. "I guess what seemed like a clever idea really wasn't. I hope you'll forgive me."

She nodded, but was afraid if she spoke she'd burst into tears. After a long pause, she finally managed to say, "It's all right."

"Listen, if you'd like to take the limo back to the hotel, it's okay with me. I have to close this place down. Then I'll walk back. I could use the air."

"I'll ask the driver to wait."

"No, don't bother. Really. Go on back." Then he gave her a sad smile. "I've been looking forward to this walk down memory lane, if you'll forgive the cliché, so I'll take a few minutes and do it alone."

Dina wanted to say more, but she couldn't find the words. She felt sorry for Michael. But pity wasn't what he wanted. The best thing she could do was leave, and so she did.

As she was riding down in the elevator, Dina let her head fall back against the side of the car. How often had she been in it? A thousand times? It smelled the same. Michael had struck a responsive chord—much more than he realized. But she did have to get away. Of that she was very sure.

By the time the car reached the ground floor tears filled her eyes and a lump had formed in her throat. She was running from a dream she thought she'd abandoned a long, long time ago. And in spite of everything that had happened—all the years that had passed—she was coming to realize that dream still had her tightly in its grip.

8

DINA WATCHED THE SUN setting over Puget Sound as she sat curled up on the sofa, the bittersweet moments of the day still haunting her. Seeing her apartment, practically as it had been five years earlier, had done it to her. Michael's ploy had cut into her soul like a surgeon's knife. She was badly shaken, as much by the way it had affected her as by the incident itself.

Did it mean she didn't love Mason, after all? No, that made no sense. Of course, she loved him. Michael had simply loosened all the deep feelings she'd repressed. But that was the past, not the future. She told herself that, over and over again.

Despite what had happened, she didn't hate Michael for having done it. To the contrary, she felt sorry for him; sorry for them both. Perhaps he'd suffered more than she'd realized. In any event, she should have seen this coming. It was stupid to have agreed to do a film with him in the first place. She should have returned to London with Mason—for Michael's sake as much as her own.

She took a deep breath. The muscles in her back and neck were in huge knots. She considered calling for a massage, but opted for a long soak in the tub. It was a good way to unwind.

She had undressed and was running the bath when there was a knock on her door. She wondered if it could be Michael. There was no one else in the crew who'd likely show up uninvited. She quickly slipped on her bathrobe and went to the door.

"Who is it?"

"Room service, Miss Winters."

"I didn't order anything," she said through the door.

"It was ordered for you by somebody else, then," the man replied.

Dina looked through the peephole. She could see a uniformed room-service waiter standing in the hall with a tray. She opened the door.

"Two prime-rib dinners," he said.

"*Two?*"

"Yes, ma'am."

"Well, I don't understand—" But then she did understand. Every time they closed a play Michael would take her to a steak house downtown to celebrate. They always had prime rib and a bottle of wine. She saw there was a bottle of cabernet on the tray. "All right, come on in." She closed the door behind him.

"Shall I set everything up for you?" the waiter asked.

"Yes, why not."

The man set the meal on the table and opened the wine to breathe. Dina tipped him and he went to the door. Opening it, she found Michael standing in the hallway. The waiter glanced back at her, then went down the hall, leaving Michael where he stood.

For a moment she stared at him. He stared back.

"I didn't want you to go hungry," he said. "And on the off chance you weren't feeling too hostile toward me, I ordered for two."

"So I see."

"We *had* planned to have dinner together."

"And you remembered I like prime rib," she said.

"Well, it is a closing night. Of sorts."

It was for her, but she had doubts he truly saw it as such. She hesitated. "I was about to take a bath. I wish you'd called me first."

"I didn't want to give you a chance to say no."

"The way you've been behaving, I'm not sure it would have fazed you anyway."

He smiled faintly. "I see my reputation precedes me."

Dina put her hands on her hips and shook her head. "Michael Cross, you are enough to drive a woman crazy. What do I have to do to convince you of my feelings?"

"I don't know. In the meantime we can't stop eating. Life goes on. And unless we get to it, that beef will get cold." He gave her his "sincere" look. "Let me apologize while we're having dinner."

"I don't want an apology."

"Well, I want to eat. One out of two isn't bad."

"All right," she said, resigned, "come on in. But only to have dinner."

Michael closed the door. "That's all you'd agreed to in the first place. And, if nothing else, I'm a man of my word."

"But your interpretation of what you've promised is extremely liberal."

"Then you've forgiven me?" he asked.

"No, but I'm sure it doesn't matter a lot to you, Michael, whether I have or not." Dina went to the table and he helped her with her chair.

Before he sat down, he lit the candle the waiter had set on the table. Then he turned off the lights in the room.

"I assume that's so you can see the view more easily," she said.

"My fondest memories are of you by candlelight."

"Comments like that don't inspire confidence."

"I'm being brutally honest, Dina."

"You have been from that day I first went to your house to talk about the film—*brutal* being the operative word."

He poured the cabernet, then picked up his glass in a toast. "To forgiveness," he said.

"No, let's make it to acceptance. Acceptance of things as they are."

"How about to compromise?"

"All right. I won't quibble. To compromise."

They each took a sip of wine. Michael removed the metal cover from each of their plates.

"*Bon appétit,*" he said.

"I can't believe I'm sitting here in my bathrobe, having dinner with you."

"Don't think anything of it. Formal dress is optional."

They began eating. Michael was pleasant and chatted amiably. Dina was less forthcoming. She was on a slippery slope, inches from disaster, and yet, she'd done nothing to prevent putting herself in this situation, except to protest mildly. Michael had to be pressing ahead because he sensed her ambivalence. Why was she letting this happen? And why didn't she put an end to it now?

When they'd finished eating, Michael leaned back in his chair, observing her closely. He stroked his chin. "You don't look like a happy camper, Geraldine Winterhalter. You seem troubled."

"I don't know why I'm letting you do this, Michael, if you want a perfectly honest answer. I tell you one thing, but I do another. I love Mason—forgive me for mentioning him—and have absolutely no doubt about that. Yet here I am, having dinner with you in a hotel room in my bathrobe."

"We're hardly strangers."

"That's the point. You're sure to get the wrong idea."

"Maybe that *is* the point, Dina."

"You're saying subconsciously I want to encourage you?" She shook her head. "Come on, Michael, I'm not a frustrated adolescent ruled by her hormones."

"Sex wasn't all we shared."

"I don't love you anymore," she said.

"No, that's not quite accurate. You don't *want* to love me anymore. There's a difference."

"I suppose I can't blame you for thinking that," she said, looking out at the view, "considering the way I've acted. I've sent mixed signals, I know. But you certainly aren't making it easy for me."

"It's not that difficult to explain," he said. "You wonder if the old magic is still there. Your rational mind tells you it shouldn't be, but in your heart you just aren't sure. I know, because I'm the same way."

"So, you've got it all figured out."

He nodded.

"I suppose you've got the solution to our dilemma all worked out, too."

He nodded again.

"Tell me, Michael, how do we resolve this?"

"Very simple, really. We give it a whirl and see how it feels."

Dina laughed. "You want me to have an affair with you, and that's supposed to clarify everything and make me feel better?"

"I don't see why not."

She put down her napkin and got up. She went to the window and looked out at the lights on the sound. "You're no better than a teenage boy trying to talk a girl into having sex," she said. "Adults don't experiment that way. I feel foolish even talking about it like this."

He got up and went over to stand behind her. Dina could see his reflection in the dark glass. He hadn't touched her, but the energy radiating from him was so intense her body began to tingle. She had a mental image of herself beginning to slip down that slope, clawing for a grip, but finding nothing to cling to.

After what seemed like forever, Michael put his hands on her shoulders. She trembled at his touch. He said nothing. In the glass she saw his head move forward and tilt to the side as first his warm breath washed over her neck, then his lips lightly touched her skin.

She closed her eyes, swallowing hard as he kissed her again and again. She groaned as his moist tongue flickered lightly up the side of her neck and back down again.

"Let's give it a try and see what happens," he whispered into her ear. "It's the quickest way to find out how we really feel."

"You're a bastard, Michael," she said as her heart tripped faster and faster. "A first-class bastard."

"I've got to know," he replied, kissing her temple. "And I think you do, too."

Dina turned and faced him. "You're being selfish. You don't have anyone else you love, but I do."

"If you're right, this will be the best way to prove it to yourself," he said. "Afterward, you'll know for sure." He caressed her jaw.

"If you loved me, you wouldn't put me through this."

"*I* made a terrible mistake in letting you get away. I don't want *you* to make one by not giving me a second chance. For both our sakes."

Words of protest were forming on her lips, but he kissed her. At first she resisted, knowing her only chance was to stop now, before it was too late. But her willpower faded. Her body knew his too well. The feel of his lips, the way he kissed, the instant excitement he invariably provoked. The intervening years disappeared from memory. The old magic took over. She wanted him.

Michael carried her to the bedroom. There was no point in resisting, no point in even thinking about it. They would make love.

He put her on the bed and kissed her. His scent, his feel, his touch, the taste of him, overwhelmed her. All that was left of her was her sexual energy, her desire. She kissed him back, wanting him as much as she ever had.

AS THEY KISSED, Michael felt her fire. It was as strong as ever. Dina moaned as she dug her fingers into his hair, her body writhing under him. A surge of excitement went through him. At last, he had her in his arms again.

He slipped his hand inside the opening of her robe, cupping one breast, adoring the feel of her. He loved her breasts, the smoothness of her skin. Just touching her was an erotic experience.

When he rubbed his thumb over her nipple, it hardened. Her tongue swept his mouth and her nails dug into his shoulders. Her excitement aroused him further. He wanted her even more.

"Michael," she moaned into his lips. "Oh, Michael."

He kissed her more fiercely still, his passion starting to lurch out of control. She could do that to him, more than any woman he'd ever known. They were like two chemicals, harmless apart, explosive when mixed together.

His loins had become a knot, swelling so hard it hurt. He couldn't breathe fast enough. And every breath was filled with her scent; the taste of her was in his mouth. She infused his body, but he couldn't get enough. He would have swallowed her if he could.

Dina rolled on top of him. She broke her mouth free of his and pressed her face into his neck, biting at the skin, holding herself back just enough not to hurt him. Then he rolled back on top of her, the weight of his body trapping her. He could feel his erection pressing into her hollow. He wanted to enter her, to take her.

"I hate you, Michael," she said breathlessly. "I hate you for this." Then she kissed him again.

He loosened her robe, moved his hand down over her belly, taking control. His fingers followed the curve of her hip, then up the inside of her leg. Dina drew taut. When he touched her mound, she was moist and warm and ready. He could feel her flesh faintly pulsing. She wanted him.

Dina closed her legs on his hand, squeezing it hard. Then she turned her head away from him, her breath coming in a rush, her chest heaving. She relaxed her legs after a while, inviting him to arouse her further. When he drew his finger over her nub, she flinched. He began caressing her and she purred at his touch.

He looked at her face. Her eyes were closed, her head turned slightly away from him. She was in her ecstasy. He liked this best. Watching her take pleasure from him was the greatest gift of all. Nothing was better than to satisfy.

Her body had forgotten nothing. Nor had his. He remembered every idiosyncrasy—what she liked best, what really turned her on.

He couldn't believe she'd found pleasure like this with Mason Fellows. And he was sure that was why she was with him now. No other two people could give each other such pleasure. Why had she fought him so?

The tremors continued to ripple through her body. He kissed her breast, running his tongue back and forth over her nipple. Dina put her hand on his, to stop him from caressing her.

"I'm going to come," she whispered, opening her eyes. "I don't want to yet, not until you're in me."

He liked that. He liked it when they came together, though it wasn't essential. But there was something so very special about giving and receiving simultaneously. One fed on the other.

He rose to his knees and began unbuttoning his shirt. Dina's eyes shone with emotion. There was a languid, vaguely yearning expression on her face. It said more than words. It was ignorant of the past and cared nothing about the future. All that mattered was now. This moment.

When he'd tossed his shirt aside, Dina reached up and unbuckled his trousers. She pulled them down, then his shorts. She looked at his penis unabashedly, taking it in her hand. Her fingers felt cool. Then, in a husky whisper, she said, "Take me, Michael. Make love to me. Do it now."

He moved between her legs and slowly lowered himself. Her breasts felt cool against his skin. And when he kissed her, he felt such love, such a well of affection, that it surprised him. The love he felt was even stronger than his desire, his need for her. "I've waited for this moment for so long," he whispered. "To be with you, to have you."

Dina did not reply. She arched against him, opening her legs. Desire surged through him and he pressed into her. He watched her face. She smiled slightly and so did he. He was in her at last, inside the woman he loved. He continued looking at her as he began moving in and out.

Once again, Dina was lost in her pleasure. Her lips trembled. When he pressed deeper her eyes widened. He felt her nails dig into his buttocks as she urged him to go faster. Her lids drooped as they moved faster and faster. He could tell her orgasm was close. His own excitement grew. It was only a matter of moments.

"Michael, Michael," she cried desperately.

Then, when she arched against him, crying out, he groaned, losing himself, erupting violently. She writhed under him for a minute or more until her orgasm had run its course. Finally she lay still.

He felt blissfully numb, complete and at peace. He savored the sensation. Then, after what seemed like an eternity, he felt her fingers in his hair. He let her caress him for a long while, finally lifting his head to look into her eyes.

"You haven't lost your touch," she murmured.

"Nor have you."

Dina rolled her head to the side, staring in the direction of the dark window. He saw sadness in her face. Her mood seemed completely at odds with what had happened. This wasn't nostalgia, it was something else.

He traced the line of her lip with his fingertip, hoping to bring her mind back from wherever it had wandered. She was so beautiful. He adored her. How long he'd dreamed of this, often doubting it would ever happen, fearful he'd lost her forever.

He could think of nothing better than being joined like this, sharing the quiet tenderness of lovers. This was the way it had been, and it was the way it should be forever.

"I love you, Dina," he whispered. "I love you so very much."

She turned back to him. There was alarm on his face. She shook her head. "Don't, Michael," she said. "Don't love me."

He was caught completely by surprise. "What do you mean?"

She pushed on his shoulder, indicating she wanted him to come out of her. He eased off her, propping his head on his arm so he could see her face.

"Dina, what's the matter?"

"I don't want you to love me," she replied.

"But why? After what we just shared. You enjoyed it, didn't you? Or was I hallucinating?"

"Oh, it was great, all right. You're a fabulous lover. The best I've ever known. There's no question about that."

"But that's still not good enough, apparently."

"Sex is wonderful, but it's not everything."

"So, that's all this was. Sex. Is that what you're saying?"

There was consternation on her face. "Of course not! I didn't ask you here to make love with me. But I was weak and I gave in. I'm not blaming you. I let it happen. I wanted you. But that's not the issue."

He stared at her, shaking his head. "So, you're saying we were just getting our rocks off? You're saying it's over, so now we can forget about it and go about our business?"

"What do you expect me to say, Michael?" she said angrily, her voice rising. "Do you expect me to abandon my life, forget the man I love, the person I am, and walk away from everything because you made me come?"

"For God's sake, Dina, this wasn't just sex. I don't care what you say. I could feel your love. Why are you denying it?"

She got up, grabbing her robe and putting it on. She cinched the tie snugly about her waist. "If I'd known you were going to be this way, I wouldn't have let it happen, no matter how much I wanted you."

He sat up, incredulous. "I can't believe you're saying this. You're not being honest with me—or yourself, either."

Dina bit her lip. "I don't want to get into a big argument with you, Michael. You thought all we had to do was make love and everything would become clear. Well, I bought your argument. Maybe you were right. I wasn't sure and I had to find out. But now I realize I was right all along—right about what's important and what's not. This wasn't me you made love with."

"Well, who the hell was it?"

"I was playing out a fantasy. I was experimenting, testing myself."

He couldn't believe what he was hearing. What was wrong with her? Was she afraid to admit all the old feelings were there? Was it her pride? Was she being stubborn to prove a point? He could win her body, but she wouldn't surrender her heart. Was that it?

"Say whatever you wish, Dina, I don't buy it. If you want the honest truth, I don't buy your love for Mason, either. One look at the two of you and I knew you didn't belong together."

"I'm sorry you feel that way. I would have preferred that you accept my love for him."

"*Love?* How can you talk about loving him after being with me?"

"Dammit, Michael, don't do this! Do you think I feel good about myself? Do you think I'm proud of what I just did?"

He shook his head. "I swear I don't understand you."

"Maybe that's the point."

"And Mason would? Are you saying he'd approve of this?"

There was fire in her eyes. "How can you do this to me?"

"I'd say you did it to yourself. It's beginning to look like I was just along for the ride."

She turned away. "You're probably right. It was self-ish of me to make love with you. I was testing my feelings without regard to you."

"That doesn't ring true, Dina. You could say it all night and I still wouldn't believe you. You're either lying or you're deceiving yourself. I don't know which is worse."

"I'm sorry you feel that way. I'm sorry it's come to this. But I can't let your opinion bother me. I have to do what I have to do."

He got up and began dressing.

"So tell me," he said, zipping his pants, "what happens now? Are you proposing we pretend this never happened?"

"That probably would be best."

"Easy come, easy go," he said sardonically. "If you forgive the pun."

She ignored his attempt at humor. "You think I'm callous and insensitive, I know. But I'm not heartless. I did learn something tonight, Michael. And you were right about one thing. This was something we had to do. Hopefully it will be easier for us now."

"We got it out of our system, in other words. Now we can be friends. Is that what I'm hearing?"

She turned to face him. "Would that be so terrible?"

He finished buttoning his shirt, then he slipped on his socks and shoes. They exchanged long looks.

"No, Dina, maybe you're right. Friendship may be the only thing we have now. But remember this—it was your choice. I stand by what I said. You know how I feel about you. Nothing you say can change that."

He waited, but she didn't respond. Tears glossed her eyes, but she refused to speak. Knowing there was nothing more to be said, he turned and walked from the room.

9

DINA LAY AWAKE for a long time after Michael had gone, worrying about the future. He hadn't regarded their lovemaking as sex, pure and simple. She'd felt the love, too, but she was confident it was love of the *memory* of what they had once shared, not love for Michael himself. At least she'd managed to keep a perspective on things. She could be thankful for that.

Then, too, there was a slim possibility that some good might come of it. Michael could no longer claim she hadn't given him a chance. She'd done it. She'd satisfied what curiosity she had. And now it was over.

She could tell he'd been shocked that she could make love with him that way and still resist him. He didn't realize that she'd been able to separate what was happening physically from what was in her heart. She didn't like to think all she'd done was have sex with him, but that's exactly what it was.

The worst part was knowing that she didn't attain the same satisfaction, the same physical joy, with Mason. The poor man simply wasn't the lover that Michael was, and in the back of her mind that did bother her. She was very sexual. She'd always been in tune with her body, comfortable with it. One of Michael Cross's great virtues was that he'd been in tune with it, as well.

When she thought about their lovemaking, a tremor went through her body. Michael was a good lover, there was no denying it. But pleasurable as sex could be, it wasn't everything. That was the point. What she shared with Mason was so much more important.

A wave of guilt washed over her then. She didn't like having to rationalize her convictions, but she knew that was exactly what she was doing. Poor Mason. The only way to rectify it was to rise above what had happened. She had to focus on Mason.

Dina glanced at the luminous dial of the clock. It was just past eleven. That made it after seven in the morning in London, too early to call under normal circumstances, but these weren't normal circumstances. In any case, Mason was an early riser. Most likely, he was having his tea and reading the *Guardian* at this very moment.

On an impulse, Dina picked up the phone and dialed Mason's flat. He answered, sounding chipper and very much awake.

"Dina, love," he said, "how terribly ironic. I was thinking about you the very moment the telephone rang."

"Something good, I hope."

"Is there anything but good?"

"Of course, there is."

"Not when it comes to you, my darling," he said. "How are you, anyway? How are things going with Cross?"

There was no suspicion in his voice, but the question stabbed at her heart just the same. Shame enveloped her.

All her rationalizing broke down with that one innocent question. She felt awful.

"Okay. Things are going well," she mumbled, compounding her misery with a lie.

"I'd hoped things were going swimmingly," he said. "The better Cross's mood, the smoother things should go with *Green September*."

The cruel irony of his remark, however innocently made, cut deeply. What would Mason say if he knew? Would she be wise to keep it a secret from him forever? Could she, and still regain a semblance of honor?

"Don't worry about *Green September*," she said. "I'm sure it will be fine."

"That's good news," he said cheerfully.

Dina closed her eyes, seeing more clearly than ever what a terrible mistake she'd made. Commitment and perfect freedom simply weren't compatible. Her only hope was that she could right the wrong she'd done.

She got Mason chatting about his film. Preproduction was going well, he said. He was happy. Fortunately he didn't get overly sentimental or go on at length about his feelings for her. He said goodbye with a simple, sweet expression of love. Dina hung up and began to cry.

MICHAEL DID NOT appreciate stubbornness, and stubbornness was exactly what he was getting from Dina. She seemed determined to thwart him—regardless of her true feelings, regardless of the proof that their love was alive and well. The best strategy was probably not to fight her. If she wasn't spending all her energy resisting him, maybe she'd start seeing things as they really were.

Right after breakfast, the crew gathered in the lobby, waiting to be bused to location. Michael greeted Dina pleasantly, but he didn't linger. He moved on to talk to Alex and Natalie. When it was time to leave, he let Dina ride alone in the limo, saying he wanted to go over some technical matters with Alex.

The first shoot was at Green Lake, in an older residential area in the north-central part of the city. The technicians had gone out earlier and set up the equipment. While Alex made adjustments in the positioning of the cameras and fretted over the fog that was rolling in from the sound, Michael strolled over to where Dina stood talking to Natalie. Dina had the collar of her trench coat turned up and was rubbing her hands together. There was a hint of apprehension in her eyes as he approached.

"You can sit in one of the vans, Dina, if you're cold," he said.

"I'm all right."

"We'll do the shots of you running first. It'll help to warm you up." As he said it, he smiled, but he was remembering the night before—the taste of her mouth, the feel of her naked body writhing under his. He didn't allow himself to linger on the thought for long. Better he convey indifference.

"At least I won't have to do it in a bikini."

"No," he said, sardonically. "We're striving for refinement this time around." Winking at Natalie, he walked on.

Fifteen minutes later he returned with his clipboard, showing Dina where she would be running and the sequence of shots they'd be taking. He took her to her mark. They began with a series of close-ups. Next came some short scenes involving Dina and minor characters. There wasn't a lot of dialogue.

Around noon it began misting. They took a break in hope that it would clear up so they could finish their work at that location. He had kept things businesslike, striving to be friendly toward Dina, but not familiar. When everyone was ready to repair to the vans for the catered lunch, he asked Natalie to take care of Dina while he joined Alex in another vehicle.

By late afternoon they'd managed to complete everything on the shooting schedule for that site. The crew began packing up the gear. He decided to ride back in the limo with Dina, but he only discussed the film and the next few days' work. When they reached downtown and were near the hotel, Dina broke the silence that had fallen between them.

"Michael," she said, "I want you to know I appreciate your professional attitude and sticking to business."

"It's nice working with an actress who doesn't let personal matters get in the way," he replied easily. "After all, we *are* here to make a film."

"You could be a bastard about it, but you haven't been. I'm grateful and wanted to tell you so."

He smiled amiably. "I promised you nothing would happen unless you wanted it to happen, and I'm a man of my word."

They arrived at the hotel and the doorman helped Dina out. He followed. They entered the lobby.

"I trust you neither expect nor want a lot of handholding," he said as they gathered their room keys from the clerk, "because I'm going to be spending my evenings working on *Green September*. I've been talking to

Rob Sharp and his agent, and I have a list of items to go over with Mason."

For the first time that day Dina's look became engaging, her eyes rounding slightly. "Do you think you'll be able to work things out with Rob? I know Mason's eager to have him play Stephen."

They started walking toward the bank of elevators.

"I don't know. The chemistry between Stephen and Clarice is as important in that film as the chemistry between Alice and Link is in this one. Considering the money I've got tied up in it, I don't want to make any mistakes."

"I'm sure Mason doesn't, either."

"You've never worked with Rob, have you?" he asked, as they waited.

"No, but I'm familiar with his work. Mason likes him a lot."

He nodded as they entered a car. "It may work out."

As they went up he glanced at her. Dina seemed self-conscious. It was their lovemaking. He could see it on her face.

"Tomorrow, if the weather holds, we'll shoot down at the waterfront. The first rainy day we'll do interiors, including the sex scene."

"All right."

"I've been thinking how I want to handle it and I may want to make some changes."

"Oh?"

They arrived at their floor and stepped out of the elevator. The doors closed behind them. Dina looked at him, waiting for an explanation.

"I've decided to be a little less graphic and go with just a suggestion of sex. Sometimes less is more. Besides, this is an action film essentially."

"You're the boss," she said. "But I hope you aren't changing things because of me. I signed on to do this film the way you want it done."

"Yes, I know. But I realized that in planning the sex scene originally I was thinking of the actress, not the character. And I have to think about Alice. Link doesn't need to be in bed with her, thrashing about stark naked, for the film to work. Save your sexual energy for Clarice and Stephen."

"Whatever you say."

"Have a nice dinner this evening," he said. "Get a good rest. We start bright and early tomorrow."

"Yes, I will."

There was a hint of wistfulness in her voice. He gave her a sly wink, then headed off toward his suite at the opposite end of the floor. He would have much preferred they were heading to the same suite, but before that could happen, Dina had an education process to endure, and he, it seemed, had to dish out a dose of tough love.

DINA SPENT THE BALANCE of the week working hard on the film by day and doing her best to relax by night. She phoned Mason almost every evening, which he referred to as his breakfast call. After a few days, they seemed not to have a great deal to talk about, but she still felt she needed to connect with him. Once again, he'd become her last line of defense against Michael.

Not that the danger was imminent—or even overt. Just the opposite. Michael didn't act indifferently toward her, but then neither did he flirt nor turn on the charm. He didn't even seem to lust after her from afar.

She was relieved, of course, and should have been glad, but oddly, it bothered her. No pressure from him was almost as bad as constant pressure. Passive-aggressive behavior. That's what it was. But how did a person complain about that? She didn't. If she were smart, she'd simply count her blessings and move on.

But Dina couldn't. Every night when she climbed into bed, Michael was in her thoughts. It didn't matter if she'd been talking to Mason only moments earlier. And it made her damned mad—angry with Michael, angry with herself, and angry with Mason for not filling her heart so completely, there was no room for a former lover. The trouble was, Michael was eating away at her happiness.

Toward the end of the week she became snappish, growling and grumbling at everyone on the set. She was being a bitch, and she knew it. For the most part, Michael ignored her unpleasantness, though he would give a look from time to time.

The day they did the sex scene she was in a particularly foul mood. Michael wanted a few shots of them in bed. The nudity was limited. She only had to be bare from the waist up and was mostly covered with a sheet, but she felt very defensive, anyway. After one aborted take, Michael told everyone to take five minutes.

Dina raised herself on her elbow and called to the wardrobe assistant to bring her robe, but Michael motioned the girl away and made Dina turn to face him.

"What's the matter?" he said in his paternal, director's voice.

"I'm not having my period," she snapped, "if that's what you're thinking."

"I didn't say you were. I'm just curious why you're upset."

She dropped down on the pillow, holding the sheet snugly over her chest, and stared up at the ceiling. "I don't know," she said. "I guess I'm not in a very sexy mood, that's all."

"Is it my imagination, or are you feeling hostile toward me?"

"It's not you."

"Then what is it?"

"Don't you think I'd tell you if I knew?" she retorted. The words had no sooner passed her lips than she knew she was out of line. "I'm sorry, Michael. I didn't mean to be so sharp. I can't explain my feelings. I guess I don't know what's going on, myself."

"I was afraid it was being in bed with me."

"No, that's not it."

"I've been trying to make it as easy for you as possible."

She thought for a minute. "Maybe underneath it *is* you—not that you've done anything wrong—it's just that I'm having trouble letting go."

"It's a little late to recast your part, so maybe we can find the secret to getting you in the mood."

She looked at him warily, but he didn't have the sardonic, suggestive little grin she expected. He had a perfectly straight face.

"I have to put everything from my mind and act."

"You're the finest actress I know, Dina."

His sincerity gave her a warm feeling. He was speaking as a director, not as a lover, and that was good. She peered into his eyes. It was the first time she'd allowed herself to *really* look at him since they'd made love. Suddenly she had a tingly feeling in her gut. Michael had said nothing, he'd just looked at her; but she knew in her heart that it would be all right.

"I think I'll be able to do it now," she said softly.

He gave her a crooked smile. "You like this guy Link quite a bit," he said. "He's about to give you the night of your life."

She nodded, repressing a smile. "If I really use my imagination, I can relate to that."

"Glad to see my directing skills aren't totally without effect. But then, it helps to have an actress with a vivid imagination." Winking, he called the crew back and they resumed shooting.

That night, in reflecting on the day, Dina realized that after the chat with Michael her problem had changed. Instead of having trouble getting herself in the mood, she'd had to struggle to hold herself back. If there hadn't been seven or eight other people in the room, something unconscionable might have happened. She had her good fortune to thank that all the sex scenes were finished now. Another day in Seattle, a few more in the studio in L.A., then she would be off to London. And her troubles would be behind her.

10

Dina checked the bathroom to make sure she hadn't missed anything, then shut her last suitcase. When she took it to the front door she noticed that Kit, who'd gotten in from New England the night before, was fertilizing the houseplants. Since Dina was preparing to leave for London that afternoon, they'd hardly had time to say a word to each other.

"I hope the plants survived my care," Dina said. "I gave them all a good soaking before I left for Seattle, and I watered them as soon as I got back."

"They need a bit of plant food, but otherwise they're fine," Kit replied. She stepped back to look at Dina, who wore a blue wool-crepe suit and low heels. "You realize we're like ships passing in the night?"

Dina smiled. "I'll be back again soon, don't worry."

Kit, who had thick, streaky blond hair, put down the bottle of plant food and turned to her, her hands on her hips. She was quite tall, and in great shape, though she rarely worked in front of the camera anymore, only occasionally taking a role in one of Barry's films. Most of the time she worked as Barry's production assistant. She wanted them to be a team, saying if they couldn't do it in real life—in marriage—they ought to be able to do it in their art.

"Well, tell me about *Cold Hearts*," she said. "What do you think? Does Michael have another smash hit on his hands?"

Dina shrugged. "It's hard to say. I haven't even seen the dailies."

"Well, Michael hasn't faltered yet, and this film, more than any of his others, must have been a labor of love."

"Why do you say that?" Dina asked without turning around.

"The leading lady."

Dina glanced back at her, but said nothing.

"How was it, working with him after all this time?"

"Not easy."

"I'd be surprised if it had been. Michael is sexy, no way around that." Kit hesitated. "I bet he wouldn't let you forget it, either."

Dina rolled her eyes. "Tell me about it. At times the sexual tension was unbearable."

"*How* unbearable?"

"You're an actress, Kit, use your imagination."

"You slept with him?"

Dina grimaced. She went over to the big wicker chair and sat down, crossing her legs. "Yes. Only once, but it was enough."

Kit smiled, but it was a sympathetic smile. "The old magic got to you, huh?"

"I put a stop to it, but not until I'd thoroughly humiliated myself."

"Surely Michael didn't rub your nose in it. That wouldn't be like him."

"No, once I made my feelings clear he backed off. But the damage was done."

"It's no reason to slit your throat," Kit said. "There's not a woman in the world who wouldn't understand the temptation. Besides, the two of you weren't exactly strangers."

"That's not the point. I should have known better. I should have been thinking about Mason."

"If it was just a fling, there's no reason to feel guilty." Kit sat in the wing chair. "It *was* just a fling, wasn't it?"

"Of course. I could never see Michael again and it would be all right." Dina looked at her watch. Ironically, Michael was due at any moment. He had some papers he wanted her to take to Mason and this had seemed like the best time to give them to her.

"Then you don't have a problem," Kit said. "No real harm was done."

"That's what I'd like to think."

"You have doubts?"

Dina shifted uncomfortably. The truth was, she was very confused—not so much about Michael as Mason. How did she square her feelings for him with everything that had happened? "I'm not sure what to tell Mason," she said.

"Don't tell him anything. If it was a fling, why muddy the water?"

"I've been trying to convince myself of that, but for some reason it just won't go down." She shook her head. "He still doesn't know anything about Michael and me having a past. The poor thing is blissfully ignorant."

"I'd leave it at that, if I were you."

Dina drummed her nails on the arm of the chair.

"It seems demeaning to keep him ignorant. It's somehow emasculating."

Kit looked at her quizzically.

"It's bad enough I was playing around behind his back," Dina went on, "but to make him the fool on top of it . . ."

Kit studied her. "Look, this is probably none of my business, but are you sure about your feelings for Mason?"

"What do you mean?"

"Well, to tell you the truth, whenever you talk about him you seem sort of tentative."

"You're mistaken. Mason and I have a wonderful relationship."

"Sexually?"

"Not all men are stallions, you know. Mason's a considerate lover. That's the most important thing when you come right down to it."

Kit looked at her thoughtfully, a long, beautifully manicured nail resting on her cheek. "Are you sure about that?"

"Absolutely."

"Far be it from me to say otherwise. You know your feelings better than I do."

"Then why do you doubt?"

"We've been friends for a long time," Kit said. "You're the only person I know who's more stubborn than I am. And I'd hate to see you talk yourself into something just because you didn't want to admit you had doubts, or were wrong. Michael may not mean a thing to you. Only you know for sure. But don't use Mason to fend him off. That's my free advice for the day. Take it or leave it."

Dina recrossed her legs. "I can't imagine what I've said or done that would put ideas like that in your head."

"Maybe I'm wrong," Kit said.

"You are. I love Mason."

"Then forget I opened my mouth."

"No, I'm curious why you would think I'm using Mason."

"I shouldn't have brought it up."

"Is it because he's not the irresistible hunk Michael is?"

"No, Dina, it's a friend observing a friend. Food for thought. Now let's let it drop."

Kit wasn't making idle chatter. Dina knew something had motivated her to speak out. Was it conviction or was it something else?

It didn't appear she'd be finding out, though, because Kit was obviously sorry she'd brought the matter up. They'd always talked freely in the past, and that was probably what had induced her to speak out now. The odd thing was that Kit's misgivings had upset her.

Dina didn't want their conversation to bother her, but it did. She had a sinking feeling, a sudden crisis of confidence. She tried to tell herself she was being silly, yet at the same time she was beginning to realize there was more than a touch of doubt festering deep in her soul. Kit had made her face that.

The question, of course, was what that doubt meant. "Mason and I have been apart too long," she said, half to herself. "I need to get back to London, that's all."

"I'm sure you're right."

The doorbell rang. They both turned toward the door.

"I think that may be your last hurdle before you go off in search of marital bliss," Kit said. "Do you want to get it, or shall I?"

Dina got to her feet. "I will."

Michael was at the door, staring at her through lightly tinted sunglasses. He was damn appealing—a touch windblown, neat yet casual. Familiar shoulders, arms, thighs. Sexy. And annoyingly attractive. "Hi," she said.

Michael had looked her over as she'd regarded him. "You look great," he said.

"Thanks. Come on in."

She led the way back. Kit got up to greet Michael. He kissed her on the cheek. "Hi, lovely. How was New England?"

"Autumnal."

"Happens up there regularly, doesn't it?"

"Once a year."

"Amazing."

They laughed and turned toward Dina, who watched with a feeling of fondness for them both.

"Well," Kit said, "I've still got some unpacking to do, if you'll excuse me. We have half an hour, Dina, before we have to hit the road." She disappeared into the bedroom and closed the door.

Michael and Dina were left standing alone. He had a large manila envelope in his hand. "This is for Mason," he said.

"Oh, fine." She took it and walked over to lay it on her luggage, by the door. Then she turned to him, feeling strangely nervous. "I'm looking forward to getting back to England," she said, knowing the statement was forced the moment she said it.

"Do you consider it home now?"

"For the time being, yes. It's Mason's home."

Michael seemed stoic. "Will he be putting you to work the minute you arrive?"

"He'll give me a day to rest, I'm sure. What's the latest on Rob Sharp? Have you signed him?"

"No, I'm still working on it."

Concern filled her. "Mason won't be pleased about that. He likes having all his ducks lined up."

"We talked about it the other day. I promised to have his leading man, along with the other Americans in the cast, there by the end of the week. It's a matter of crossing a few *t*'s and dotting some *i*'s."

"Oh. Well, I'll leave that to you two to work out."

"Yes, no point in spending our last few minutes together talking shop."

There was wistfulness in his voice. Dina looked at him and a curious sadness welled inside her.

"It's a beautiful day," he said, gesturing toward the expanse of glass overlooking the sunny beach. "L.A. put on her best dress to say goodbye to you."

"So it seems."

"Would you like to walk on the beach?"

"I'm hardly dressed for it," she said, looking down at herself.

"Kit must have a pair of sneakers you can slip on."

"With this suit?"

"Funk is in."

"There's an old pair of jogging shoes on the deck. Maybe I could wear them. But if I run my panty hose, it's your fault."

"I take full responsibility."

They went out onto the deck. Dina was able to slip into the shoes easily. Michael unfastened the gate and they went down the short flight of stairs to the beach. They slogged across the soft sand to where it was firmer by the water's edge.

The breeze was light and the temperature balmy. They headed up the beach, past two boys and a yapping dog playing with a Frisbee. Dina inhaled the sea air. It was delightful.

"I must confess I'm not looking forward to winter in London," she said. "We'll probably get away to Portugal or Morocco in January to warm our bones a little."

"Do you and Mason travel well together?" he asked.

Dina pulled a wisp of hair back off her face. "Yes, I'd say we do."

"He's a lucky man, Dina. I don't have to tell you that."

"Michael, I've been wanting to say something to you and now's probably as good a time as any. Thanks for not trying to take advantage of my mistake in Seattle."

"I would have, if I could have figured out how to do it."

"Well, you didn't and I'm grateful."

"I hope that, all in all, doing *Cold Hearts* with me wasn't too unhappy an experience."

"Except for that one thing, I enjoyed it."

He grinned. "It would be kinder to my ego to have said, 'Except for that one thing, it was a terrible experience.'"

"Maybe that night was good in its way, Michael, but I'm not sure saying it is better for your ego, or our friendship."

"Odd, that it has to be one way or the other. Too bad it wasn't wonderful all the way around."

"Maybe. But it wasn't. And you know why."

"Do I read between the lines that we can still be friends?"

"Of course. I don't believe in trying to erase the past for the sake of the present. What was, was. The point is, we go on from here."

"Yes, I guess we do, don't we?"

They walked for a while in silence.

"I'll probably come over with the rest of the American contingent, Dina. The investors want me to keep an eye on their money. I hope that won't be a problem for you."

"No, why should it be?"

"I'd like to think it's not, but I wanted you to know."

"It'll be different when I'm with Mason. You didn't see the real me in Seattle, Michael."

"I'm sorry to hear that. I really am."

She glanced at him, having heard the sincerity in his voice. Michael was sad, and in a funny sort of way it touched her.

They walked to the end of the beach, then turned around and headed back. She asked about his plans for the postproduction on *Cold Hearts* and whether she thought she might be needed for any reshooting. He explained that he'd already gone over the footage carefully and hadn't found anything that involved her character, but he wouldn't know for sure until he did the final edit, when he returned from Europe.

When they got to Kit's, Michael stopped her at the foot of the stairs and took her hands. She looked into his eyes, feeling a wistful sadness.

"I'd planned never to say goodbye to you again," he told her. "Not like this, anyway."

"We both learned something about ourselves. I don't regret what happened—for that reason, if for no other. I just hope you'll look ahead now, and not back."

"I haven't been living in the past," he replied. "But I admit the past has guided the future I want. I know you don't like hearing that, but it's true." He reached up and pushed back a strand of hair that had blown across her cheek. "You'll have to forgive me for loving you."

That sad smile was on his lips again. He slowly dragged his finger down her cheek, then along the side of her neck, as if savoring the feel of her.

Dina felt an ache deep inside her and fought against it.

"I'll say goodbye now," he whispered huskily. He looked deeply into her eyes. "'Such sweet sorrow,'" he quoted. "I hate this goodbye even more than the last." Then he kissed her lips, caressing her scarcely more than the wind.

Dina stood there, her eyes closed, her face lifted slightly; his breath, the breeze and the feel of his lips, all one sensation. The moment sent her heart tripping. Then it was over. She pulled back, opening her eyes.

"Break a leg, Geraldine Winterhalter," he said. Then, touching her cheek a final time, he turned and climbed the stairs.

When he'd disappeared behind the gate, Dina sat down on a step and stared out to sea. The boys with the Frisbee and the dog were moving up the beach. Two gulls hovered above the waves. A sailboat glided across the horizon, and Dina realized she'd lost all desire to go to London.

11

IT WAS MIDMORNING as Dina stepped out the front door of her flat on Curzon Street. A taxi was pulling up. The passenger got out. He was fair, blue-eyed, good-looking. Seeing him gave her a start. It wasn't Michael, though. This man was a good deal smaller and several years older. Plus, he carried a bowler, which he popped onto his head. His Savile Row suit and brolly confirmed that he was British.

Dina's unnatural degree of awareness made him smile. A gentleman, he held the door of the taxi for her, but said nothing as she climbed in. After paying the driver, he stepped back and nodded before turning and walking away. Dina shivered as though she'd just seen Michael Cross himself.

"Where will it be, then, love?" asked the driver, an older man with a heavy gray mustache.

"Kensington. St. Mary Abbots Hospital, please."

Off they went toward Park Lane. Dina was still thinking of the start she'd had. Her reaction wasn't surprising, considering she'd thought about Michael all during her flight across the Atlantic and for most of the three days she'd been home. Even finding Mason ill and in need of constant attention hadn't been enough to get her mind off Michael.

Just when she'd hoped to spend some serious quality time with Mason, he came down with pneumonia. It wasn't too serious—"walking pneumonia" was how the doctor described it—but poor Mason couldn't go off to France to shoot his movie until he was better. Dina had persuaded him that a couple of days in the hospital, followed by a few more days of bed rest at home, was exactly what he needed.

At first he'd resisted. Then she put her foot down. "If you don't nip this in the bud," she told him, "you'll get too sick to make your film and Michael will find another director." That had brought Mason around real quick.

Dina was disappointed that they couldn't be together, but it did give her an opportunity to lounge around for a couple of days and recover from jet lag. Unfortunately it also gave her time to think about Michael. Kit's little speech had made her wonder if she was ignoring some obvious truth. God knows, it was hardly a good sign that she was trying to convince herself of the depth of her feelings for Mason.

She'd decided on the flight over to tell Mason everything. Having it hanging over her head was not doing her any good. She was confident of his forgiveness. Mason had never failed her yet.

But finding him sick, she didn't have the heart to burden him. Nor did she want to say anything on the eve of Michael's arrival. That meant she'd probably have to delay her *mea culpa* until after Michael returned to California. In the meantime, she was saddled with his ghost.

Ironically, most of her thoughts of Michael weren't sexual. It would have been easier if they had been. Instead she thought about the way he affected her emotionally.

The taxi made a circuit of Wellington Arch and entered Knightsbridge. London was familiar, but not as comfortable as it had been before her trip to California. She had been so content with her life back then; why couldn't she feel that way now?

As they went down Brompton Road, traffic came to a halt. Dina wondered why she was thinking about a man she no longer loved, when she was about to see the man she did love. Mason deserved better.

After turning on Cromwell Road they moved past the Victoria and Albert Museum at a fairly brisk pace. In a few minutes they turned onto Marloes Road and soon pulled up in front of the main entrance to the hospital. She tipped the driver generously. He saluted her and she dashed up the steps and into the reception area. Mason was sitting there waiting, with a script and shooting schedule open on his lap, his case at his feet.

"Darling, what are you doing down here?" she said, surprised to see him ready.

"I can't wait to get out of this bloody place," he replied with a wan smile.

Mason stood and they embraced.

"Being in hospital is not my cup of tea."

Dina patted his cheek. "But you look better. It was the right thing to do."

"Well, I'm eager to get home."

"I'll find us a taxi."

"I'll come along," he said.

"It's quite cool out. You shouldn't get chilled."

"There's a stand just up the street." He put on his top-coat and picked up his case. "Anyway, I've got news."

They headed for the door.

"What kind of news?"

"Cross rang me up this morning. Tracked me down through the studio."

"Oh? What did he want?" Dina asked warily.

"He's coming in advance of the others. Wants to review my plans and go over budgets before we head for France."

"That's odd," she said as they went through the door. "When's he coming?"

"Tomorrow."

"*Tomorrow?*"

"Yes," Mason said, closing his lapels over his chest as they went down the steps. "I'm just as glad. You know how keen I am on having everything in order."

They'd no sooner reached the pavement when a taxi came by. Mason hailed it. Dina climbed in the back and Mason followed, giving the driver the address of his little house, which was in Kensington, not far away.

She wasn't exactly shocked by Mason's announcement, but it had caught her off-balance. Once again, Michael had tossed a monkey wrench in the works. She couldn't help but think it was intentional.

"I was looking forward to us having some time alone," she groused.

"Cross holds the purse strings, love. Mustn't offend him."

"Well, we certainly don't have to wine and dine him."

"Not to worry. He understands we'll have to confer at my sickbed, and he wants me recovered in time to go to

France on schedule. But you can take him out to dinner,
so he won't feel neglected."

Dina looked at him with dismay. "Was that Michael's
idea?"

"No, I believe I mentioned it first. Is there a problem
with that, darling? You know the man, for heaven's sake.
It won't be grim duty. You do count him a friend, don't
you?"

"Mason, I was looking forward to spending time with
you."

"You shall, dearest. This is only for a few days while I
regain my strength." He took her hand.

Dina had a terrible sinking feeling. Michael again. She
was sure he intended to take advantage of the situation.
The moment he heard Mason was ill, he probably decided to pounce. The wily bastard.

"Well, at least we have tonight," she said.

Mason kissed her hand. "Yes, indeed."

"Maybe we should drop by a wine shop and pick up a
bottle of champagne," she said.

He gave her a sly grin. "You *have* missed me."

"Of course, I have," she replied, though with less conviction than she'd have liked. But Dina knew she had to
exorcise Michael any way she could, before it was too
late.

WHEN DINA AWOKE the next morning she listened for the
surf, only to realize she wasn't in Malibu. The realization caused anxiety. Her homecoming had not produced the great sense of relief she'd expected.

She'd ended up returning to her flat rather than
spending the night with Mason. By bedtime he'd been

too exhausted for an amorous evening, conking out on the sofa soon after dinner. He'd had a glass of champagne before admitting that the doctor advised him to avoid alcohol until he finished his course of antibiotics. So, after cleaning up, Dina had seen him off to bed, then grabbed a taxi for home.

When she checked her watch, she saw that she'd overslept. Her internal clock seemed less willing to leave California than the rest of her. Fortunately, Mason's housekeeper, Mrs. Brown, always arrived early and made him his breakfast. Dina knew he was in good hands.

She'd told him she'd come around to fix lunch, which didn't give her much time. But it wasn't Mason's stomach, or even his health, that preoccupied her; it was Michael's imminent arrival. Mason hadn't said when he expected him, but knowing Michael, it would be sooner rather than later.

By the time Dina had taken her bath, dressed and found herself a taxi, it was nearly noon. Twenty minutes later she was in front of Mason's little house. As she reached for the door knocker, she could hear laughter. It sounded like a party. She had to step back to make sure she was at the right place. There had been no mistake. She rapped on the door.

Mrs. Brown, a ruddy-cheeked Northerner, greeted her. "Ah, Miss Winters, they've been expecting you."

Dina slipped off her trench coat, tossed it on a chair, and went through the tiny entry hall to the parlor, where a group of four were gathered. There was Mason in his silk robe, seated in his favorite chair, Madhavi Young, his longtime assistant director and the only woman in the group, a tall, distinguished-looking gray-haired man Dina didn't know, and Michael Cross.

The men stood. Michael wore a navy double-breasted wool suit with a maroon Italian-silk tie. He smiled. She stared at him incredulously, curious about what was going on.

"Dina, darling," Mason said. "Just in time to have some tea with us. Come on, then, we've a cup for you."

She made her way over. Mason introduced the man Dina didn't know.

"This is Richard Reinerston, one of Michael's financial partners. Mr. Reinerston is in real estate in Sacramento."

Dina shook hands with the man. "Welcome to London."

"Pleasure to meet you, Miss Winters. My wife and I have been admirers of yours since *Mirabella*."

"Thank you, Mr. Reinerston."

"Richard wanted a close-up look at our investment," Michael said, "so I invited him and Maryly along."

"How nice. We're happy to have you," she said sweetly.

After exchanging looks with Michael, she sat on the sofa next to Madhavi, a darkly attractive woman in her forties with streaks of gray in her hair. She was originally from Bombay where she'd worked in the Indian film industry before marrying an English clergyman and settling in London. She'd been working with Mason for ten years, "tempering his excesses," as he liked to say. Madhavi had on one of the saris that she occasionally wore. Dina took her hand.

"Good to see you," she said.

"Welcome home, Dina. Was California good to you?"

"Yes," she said, with a glance at Michael. "It was like old times, being back where I got my start."

"So," Mason said, settling back in his chair, "Michael has brought wonderful news."

"Oh?" She looked at him warily, not knowing what to expect.

"It was bad news, actually," Michael said, "but we're all trying to make the best of it. Rob Sharp isn't going to do *Green September*, which leaves us in a bind. I've offered to take the role of Stephen. Mason has agreed that it would be a workable solution."

"Just agreed?" Mason said heartily. "Come on now, old man. I couldn't be more delighted. By any calculation it's a step up and brings a star quality to the film...to go with Dina's, of course."

She was incredulous. "*You're* going to play Stephen?"

"I know you've probably seen more of me than you'd care to for a while," Michael admitted, "but there's something to be said for us being paired in back-to-back films. One can feed off the other."

"I think it's marvelous," Mason said.

Dina gave him an annoyed look for being so damned cheerful about it. Didn't he realize this was a disaster?

"It can only help at the box office," Reinerston said. "After all, that's what really matters."

She looked back and forth at the three men. It was like a terrible conspiracy. Just when she thought her troubles with Michael were behind her, she was right back in the fire. She flashed him an accusing look.

"I know you were looking forward to working with Rob," he said, "but I'm sure that under Mason's direction we'll do well."

It was all Dina could do to keep from lashing out at him. What a hypocrite! He'd made sure Rob wasn't going to be in the film on purpose. No wonder he'd insisted on having the last word on casting. He'd planned this from the beginning!

She turned to Mason, hoping to find some sympathy. He was as much a victim in this as she. To her chagrin, he looked amazingly content, though she could see her reaction was starting to perplex him.

"When you think about it, love, it's a jolly good break. Michael brings not only megastar quality to the picture, but he's a terrific actor and will be a wonderful Stephen. I would have thought you'd be delighted." His brow furrowed.

"I'm sure you're right, Mason. But I have to adjust to the idea."

Mason smiled, looking relieved. Dina felt awful. And she was mad as hell at Michael.

She sat quietly as the conversation moved on. Mrs. Brown came in to pour them some tea. Dina sipped hers, but her mind was churning, trying to sort out the implications of Michael's latest move. Damn him, she wouldn't let him profit from this ploy, if it was the last thing she did.

MICHAEL LISTENED AS Mason and Madhavi Young went on and on about the schedule for the location shoot in France. The French government had been generous with their subsidies and production assistance, and were particularly eager to promote period pieces like *Green September*.

Michael looked over at Dina. She was upset by the news. He'd expected that—he'd left her without options. It had been a calculated risk. His only hope now was to make it so obvious to her that they belonged together that she couldn't deny it any longer.

God only knew what his chances were. His best shot had been in Seattle, and he'd come up short. With Mason on the scene, his task might be impossible, but he wouldn't give up without one more fight.

Half an hour had passed since Dina had arrived. She'd said just enough so as not to appear to be sulking, but he knew she was upset. Mason had been going on at length when Dina suddenly got to her feet.

"Mason, forgive me, but I'm feeling a little warm. I don't know if jet lag is bothering me more than usual or if it's nerves, but I'm going for a walk up the street, if you don't mind."

"Of course not, darling. But do you think you should go out? Maybe you should lie down for a while instead."

"No, I need some air, that's all. Excuse me," she said, glancing at everyone but him.

Dina went to the entry. As the front door opened, then closed, Mason had a vaguely distressed expression on his face.

"She's disappointed that I'll be playing opposite her," Michael said. "I think I've got some fences to mend. If you don't mind, Mason, I'll have a word with her."

"Not at all. I'm terribly sorry, old man. I can't imagine why she's so upset."

Michael excused himself and left the room. Dina was walking along the pavement only a few doors away as he descended the steps. She was holding the collar of her coat up around her ears and her head was bowed. He quickly came up alongside her.

"Can we commiserate together over this sad turn of events?" he asked.

Dina glanced at him. "Michael, what are you trying to do? Ruin my life?"

"I want to make this film with you."

"Bull. You're lying and you know it."

"All right, I'm desperately grasping at every available straw. I want to be with you any way I can, at any cost."

"At least that's honest," she said.

"Does that mean you like me again?"

She gave him a look that was unmistakably disapproving. She'd noticed he'd come outside in just his suit coat. "Michael, you'll catch your death. We can't have both the director *and* the leading man ill."

"There's no sacrifice I wouldn't make."

"Please, spare me." They continued to walk. "Tell me what you're going to do. Nothing to embarrass everyone, I hope."

"No, my plan is simply to stay close in hopes you'll eventually admit we should be together."

"You refuse to give up."

"True."

"I'm going to marry Mason."

"Not to spite me, I hope."

She stopped and faced him. "Are you really that self-centered? Why can't you accept the fact that I love him?"

"Maybe I *am* too self-centered. But I believe you're deluding yourself. I plan to be around when you discover that."

"Well, don't hold your breath."

He gave her his most endearing look, hating it that nothing he tried seemed to work. "You don't have the tiniest bit of compassion for me?"

"Yes, I do. Go back inside before you catch cold. I don't want you sick, too."

"It's a step in the right direction, I suppose," he said with an ironic grin.

She looked at him with a certain wistful sincerity. "Don't expect anything more, Michael. For both our sakes."

The words were unequivocal, but he didn't believe her. Deep inside her he was almost sure he detected a twinge of doubt, a sliver of fear. It offered very little hope, but at the moment it was all he had.

12

THAT EVENING MICHAEL took Dina and the Reinerstons to dinner at Le Gavroche. Dina was charming to them, but cool with him. He'd have preferred it the other way around, but at least they were together.

She looked absolutely lovely in a pale beige suit and diamond stud earrings, though he could tell she was tired. All the same, he stared at her half the evening, wishing he knew the secret to unlocking her heart. Seducing her hadn't worked. Somehow she'd managed to put that night in Seattle aside.

For him, the effect had been just the opposite. His love for her had become even more powerful and urgent than before. And he would prove it to her, even if it meant stealing her from Mason Fellows at the altar the way Dustin Hoffman did Katharine Ross in *The Graduate*.

In the course of the dinner conversation, the Reinerstons asked about his plans for the future. Michael told them about his theater project in Seattle.

"Do you prefer the theater to film?" Richard asked.

"Once a stage actor, always a stage actor," he replied, looking at Dina as he said it. "Personally, as well as professionally, those were my happiest days."

Dina looked down at her wineglass, refusing to meet his gaze. In answer to Maryly Reinerston's next question, he told them he would be mounting a production of *Othello* to open his new theater. After they finished filming *Green September* he would be returning to Seattle to cast it.

"How delightful," Maryly said. "Richard, we have to fly up for the opening."

The conversation moved on to London theater and some of the things Dina had done. After their coffee, Richard suggested they go to the casino, but Dina begged off, saying she was tired. She urged them to go on, but Michael said he'd see her home in a taxi.

A few minutes later they were outside the restaurant in the chilly night air. The Reincrstons were off in one taxi and he ushered Dina into another.

"This really isn't necessary," she said impatiently. "You should have gone with your friends."

"I'd rather be with you, even if it's only to ride in a taxi through the streets of London."

"Don't romanticize this," she warned. "Please, don't."

It was a short ride to Curzon Street. He had the taxi wait while he went with her to the door.

"If you'll invite me in for a brandy, I'll send the taxi away," he said hopefully.

"I'm not inviting you in, Michael."

"Well, at least I'm not having to drop you off at Mason's. That would be hard to take."

"You'd better get used to it. As soon as he's feeling better, I'll be with him." She sniffled then, taking a handkerchief from her purse and wiping her nose.

"Are you getting sick?" he asked.

"I haven't felt quite right all day. Maybe I'm fighting something."

"I'll fix you a cup of tea and tuck you into bed, if you'll let me."

Dina extended her hand pointedly. "Good night, Michael. Thank you for the lift."

He took her hands in both of his, holding them, peering into her eyes. "How do I convince you, Dina?"

She shook her head. "You don't." She slipped her hand free of his and went inside. For a few moments he just stood there. By any standard he should have been discouraged. But he wasn't. He was more determined now than ever. He knew he was right. He knew it with absolute certainty.

DINA'S SNIFFLES TURNED into a bad cold and he didn't see her for a few days. Meanwhile Mason was improving daily, and Michael spent a couple of days working with him at his house.

It was evident that Mason didn't have the slightest idea what had gone on between him and Dina, otherwise he wouldn't have been so enthusiastic about them playing opposite each other. "I want this film to be sensual," Mason said one afternoon. "If done right, it'll be the height of eroticism."

"I couldn't agree more," he replied.

"Dina's wonderfully sensuous, once she gets into a role. How did you find it, directing her?"

Michael thought for a moment. "You're right. There's a certain reserve and reticence about her until she relaxes. Once you push the right button, though . . ."

"Exactly," Mason said. "And I sense the chemistry between you two will be perfect for what I have in mind."

Michael felt a pang of guilt, but only for a moment. "I hope you're right."

By the end of the week, when the American contingent arrived and it was time to head for France, Mason had recovered from his pneumonia and Dina was starting to feel better. Michael saw her for the first time at the airport. It was early morning. She was in a heavy parka, a bulky sweater and stretch pants. She and Mason entered the VIP lounge where Caroline Stone and Bryce Heath, the principal supporting actors, and two or three other members of the cast, were waiting.

Mason stopped to talk to Madhavi Young, and Dina wandered over to say hello to the others. Finally, when it was unavoidable, she turned to him.

"Hello, Michael."

"How are you feeling?" he asked.

"Better. There's nothing worse than a head cold. In another two or three days I should be good as new."

"A new film, a new chapter."

"And a new life." She stepped closer, lowering her voice. "There's something I have to tell you, Michael. We're having a little reception this evening in Amboise before dinner. Mason and I are officially announcing our engagement. I wanted you to know and not be caught off guard."

He was stunned. In spite of the fact she'd been telling him she intended to marry Mason, he hadn't let himself believe it. Not deep inside. They exchanged long looks. He watched her face carefully. She was trying hard to be convincing, but he read a spark of uncertainty in her eyes. "It's considerate of you to let me know," he said. "Now I can prepare myself."

Dina nodded. "Yes, do."

"Would it seem too hypocritical of me to offer my congratulations?"

She shook her head. "No, but please accept the fact that I *am* going to marry him."

He didn't have another chance to talk to her. On the plane she sat in the row behind him, with Mason. They talked during most of the brief flight. He couldn't pick out more than the occasional word, but the tone had that giddy quality typical of lovers. It wasn't easy for him to take.

Once they landed, they passed quickly through customs. Most of the crew had arrived a day or two earlier, so their party was accommodated by a couple of Citroën limousines and a minibus. Bryce Heath, a good-looking man about his own age, rode with him. He considered Heath a good actor, but for some reason he'd never made it as a leading man. Caroline Stone, who'd worked with Mason before, rode with him and Dina.

Michael was in no mood to indulge in small talk and fortunately Heath was interested in sleeping. The decision had been made to drive directly to Tours in the Loire Valley, where most of the shooting would be done. The road was dry but the sky was threatening. Brisk winds whipped the branches of the trees alongside, sending leaves tumbling.

The drive only took a few hours, but they arrived at their hotel late for lunch. Most of the crew elected to have something brought to their rooms. Michael had a sandwich, then lay down to rest.

As he lay in bed, he listened to the raindrops spattering against the windowpanes. Were Dina and Mason snuggled together on their bed? If she'd been with him, he'd be telling her of his love, stroking her hair, plotting a night of lovemaking. But for a reason he couldn't fathom, Dina was clinging to Mason and resisting him at every turn.

He could only assume that the engagement business was her idea. She was forcing the issue—almost fanatically. Why? What was she afraid of?

Thunder shook the windows. Somehow it seemed to suit his melancholy mood. He sighed. "Geraldine Winterhalter," he murmured, "why are you doing this to me?"

IT WAS BARELY LIGHT the next morning as they gathered in the lobby. Dina sat in an armchair, trying to remain calm as Mason fussed with Madhavi, getting things ready for their departure. A bus was waiting to take the American and British contingent to the Château Vaumas, where the initial filming would be done. Another bus had already departed with the French production crew.

"Who are we missing?" Mason asked impatiently.

"Michael, Heath and Caroline," Madhavi answered calmly. One of her great virtues was her unwillingness to let Mason fluster her. "But they have a few more minutes. I told them seven."

Mason looked at his watch. "Caroline hates early calls. I hope she didn't oversleep." He went off to dither with something else and Dina smiled. Dear Mason.

He'd been awfully sweet when they'd announced their engagement. He'd toasted her so nicely. She'd beamed, feeling so very happy, though she hadn't been able to ignore those pale, pale blue eyes watching her from the

back of the room, amused, doubting, defying. She'd
wanted to announce their engagement to send Michael
the strongest possible message, but he'd remained un-
deterred. She could tell.

Even as she and Mason had gone to their room after
dinner, to make love for the first time in six weeks, Michael's eyes had haunted her, following her even to her
fiancé's bed.

Unfortunately Mason had had a bit too much champagne and their lovemaking had been less than stellar.
But he'd told her over and over again how deeply he
loved her. That was all she needed. Yet, for an hour after
he'd gone to sleep she lay awake, thinking of Michael.

Part of the problem had been her mother. After they
arrived the previous day, Dina had called Bernice Winterhalter in Iowa to tell her the engagement was now official.

"Congratulations, dear," her mother had said, more
with politeness than conviction.

Unfortunately, because her mother had never taken to
Mason, Dina had kept them apart. But now that they
were going to marry, it would be unavoidable. Sooner
or later, they'd have to go to Cedar Rapids to visit her.

"Apparently, doing that movie with Michael didn't
ignite any smoldering coals," Bernice had said.

"No, Mother. Michael is a thing of the past. That's
over. I hope you'll at least give Mason a chance."

Her mother hadn't argued, but her thoughts on the
matter—and her high regard for Michael—were more
than evident. Dina had known that going in.

The conversation had moved on to other subjects. Her
mother told Dina to give her regards to Mason, and then

she'd said goodbye. It wasn't until later that Dina realized she hadn't even asked when the wedding would be.

The subject of a wedding took Dina's mind back to the one she'd planned with Michael. She remembered the excitement, the joy they'd felt. If it hadn't been for that actress in the cast of *Sitting Pretty* getting pregnant, she'd be Mrs. Michael Cross at this very moment.

Michael had thought about that, too. That first day, when she'd had lunch at his house, he'd talked about the son they'd have had if it hadn't been for that call from Hollywood. He'd even reminded her of that rainy night in Seattle when he tried to get her pregnant. How young and silly they'd been. And how desperately in love.

Just then, in the middle of her thought, the elevator doors opened and Michael appeared. He was with Caroline Stone, a pale blonde with delicate features and fine bones. They were laughing. Caroline's cheeks looked rosy and she seemed happy. Dina immediately wondered if they were coming from the same room, the same bed. Jealousy shot through her.

Then she caught herself. How ironic that she was jealous of Michael the morning after she'd become engaged. The thought that he still affected her that way made her color.

Michael and Caroline walked over to where Mason and Madhavi were standing. When Michael glanced at her, Dina looked quickly away, then, thinking better of it, returned his gaze. He gave her a wink and smiled. Maybe he had finally gotten the message and decided to console himself with Caroline.

Watching them, Dina decided she was glad. If that's what it took to make him get on with his life, it was just as well. In fact, it was the best thing that could happen. Buoyed by the thought, she got up and went over to join the group. No sooner had good-mornings been exchanged than Bryce Heath stepped out of the elevator and joined the group.

"Well, *mes amis*," Mason said chipperly, "what do you say we go make a movie?"

"Not without a cup of coffee," Bryce intoned.

"There are thermoses on the coach, old man. We've thought of everything!"

Mason went off like the Pied Piper and the others fell in behind him. Michael gave Dina a wry smile.

"You look lovely this morning. Did you have a good night?"

"It was wonderful, thank you. And you, Michael?"

His only response was a coy smile.

"Good for you," she said as she went out the door ahead of him. "It's the best thing that could happen."

"What's that? What do you mean?"

She glanced over her shoulder at him and gave him a wink.

13

SINCE *GREEN SEPTEMBER* was a historical drama, the actors spent hours in wardrobe and makeup before they could begin filming. The plan was to do interior shots first, but when the weather turned sunny and crisp, Mason shuffled the schedule to shoot exteriors. They began with the scenes involving getting in and out of carriages, walking in gardens and running across fields.

Dina was relieved to finally be occupied. She took refuge in her character. Mason was totally lost in his work, and his preoccupation left her pretty much on her own when she wasn't in front of the camera.

The first three or four days of filming were spent at Château Vaumas and in the surrounding park. There were only half-a-dozen scenes involving both Clarice and Stephen. As it turned out, Dina and Caroline were in quite a few scenes together.

Dina didn't know her as well as Mason did, but she found the woman pleasant and a competent actress. Between takes they would chat or have a cup of tea together in one of the trailers. But in spite of the time they spent together, Dina couldn't decide if Caroline was sleeping with Michael or not. Whenever she observed them together, she saw no obvious sign. Caroline was reticent and didn't pick up on any of the opportunities Dina gave her to talk about Michael.

Toward the end of the week the weather turned blustery and Mason decided to shift indoors and shoot interiors. The château, modest by the standards of the Loire, was nevertheless perfect for filming. It was furnished in authentic period pieces and was available only because it was closed to the public for the season. A ministry official closely observed their work, but Mason was given great latitude in using the building.

They did a series of parlor scenes, including an extended one by the fire between Clarice and Stephen. Except for walking arm in arm in the garden, it was the first work they'd done together. Mason had them run through the entire thing before the first take. He stood watching, his hands on his hips.

"Dina, love," he said when they'd finished, "I'm not liking this much. Are you saving yourself for film, or is the costume bothering you?"

"I'm sorry, Mason, I guess I'm not into it yet. I'll try harder."

"More likely you need to relax, darling. You love this man, after all. Keep thinking how much you want him."

She glanced at Michael. He was trying not to smile.

"I would offer my assistance," Michael said, "but I'm not sure it would be well received."

"I don't need any help, thank you."

"Personally, to get into a romantic mood, all I have to do is think of Seattle."

"I'm surprised you didn't say all you had to do was think of last night."

"And why would I do that?"

"Haven't you found other outlets for your amorous impulses?"

"No."

He hadn't hesitated. Had she misread the situation?

"Evidently I was mistaken." She strolled over to the tall windows. Behind her she could hear Mason talking to the director of photography. They spoke half in French, half in English.

Outside, against the dark tangle of tree branches in the park, she noticed flakes of snow drifting down. Dina shivered and a sudden feeling of desperation came over her. She turned. Michael was staring at the fire. For some reason, she flashed on that night when he had tried to get her pregnant, confessing how badly he wanted to give her a child.

"Clarice," Mason said, his voice shattering her thoughts, "are you feeling amorous now?"

She turned to her fiancé. It took a moment to bring herself back from the daydream she'd been lost in. "Yes," she said, "I think I'm ready."

Mason stepped over and put an arm around her shoulders. "He adores you, darling. This man wants to take you away. You're resisting, but you know you'll succumb. You want him."

"Yes, Mason, I understand." Dina went and sat on the floor next to Michael.

Michael looked at her with a deep passion. Or was it "Stephen" who was gazing at her? It didn't matter. The crackling fire reminded her of that rainy night in Seattle—the hot toddies, his burning desire for her.

Michael grinned like he knew what was going on in her mind. He pinched her chin and said, "That color in your cheeks looks promising. Do you mind me asking what you thought about to get into the mood?"

"Yes, Michael, I do mind. It's none of your damned business."

"All right, people," Mason called out. "We're doing this one for the camera. Quiet, please."

A hush fell over the room. Dina could see a reflection of the flames dancing in Michael's eyes.

"Shall I tell you what *I* was thinking?" he asked softly.

"No," she murmured. "I'd rather not know."

"Ready..." Mason called out. "Camera." Then, after a pause, "Action!"

"Stephen" drew a deep breath, inhaling her scent. His mouth opened slightly. He looked at her lips. "'Clarice,'" he whispered, "'I've waited so long to be alone with you like this. It's God's will that we're together, I know it is.'"

AS THE DAYS PASSED, Michael haunted her more and more. On camera, her love affair with "Stephen" was progressing. Off camera, Michael gave her an occasional consuming look, but otherwise seemed content to let Stephen speak for him.

Mason remained obsessed with his film, which kept her at a distance from him. They would have dinner together, but he could talk of nothing but *Green September*. It particularly galled her when he spoke highly of Michael's work, his talent. Couldn't he see what it was Michael really wanted? How could Mason be so blind?

For most of a week they shot in Tours and Angers. They did a passionate scene in the Cathedral of St. Maurice where Stephen professed his love, begging Clarice to go off with him. They'd done the scene so well that Mason was happy with the first take. Michael's eyes had shone with emotion as he said his lines. And she was greatly moved, just as the script called for her to be.

It was the middle of December and they still hadn't done the climactic love scene that was central to the film. Mason wanted to hold back and do it toward the end. Michael had asked that his scenes be completed as early as possible so he could leave a week before the rest of the cast, all of whom hoped to be home for the holidays.

Mason agreed; he was especially sympathetic, knowing Michael had to cast and rehearse a play in time for a February opening. In fact Mason was particularly solicitous toward Michael not only because he was financing the picture, but also because his name could very well make the film. To Dina, this was all bitterly ironic.

When an unexpected snowstorm blew in, blanketing western France, Mason decided to take advantage of the opportunity to reshoot a few critical scenes at Château Vaumas and to do the love scene, which would wrap up Michael's work on the film.

By ten o'clock the next morning "Stephen" and "Clarice" were arriving at the château as the snow fell in large soft flakes. They were greeted by a servant and rushed into the building. Most of the intervening scenes had already been shot, but Mason redid two, to take advantage of the snowy vista through the windows.

All that remained was the love scene, which had been written into the script as sensual and graphic. Dina had dreaded this day—it would be the acid test of her abilities.

First Mason had her undress by the window with the snowy backdrop of the park rendering her in silhouette. He'd agreed to her request to keep the number of crew present to an absolute minimum. But he wanted Michael there.

"In your mind, Stephen is watching, love," he said.

The terrible irony of Mason's remarks cut into her soul, but Dina knew she had to bear up. She undressed twice before Mason was satisfied. And because of the draftiness of the château, she was shivering before they were done.

"I'll probably look blue on film," she said as she slipped into the robe the wardrobe assistant brought to her.

"This place was no better heated two hundred years ago, darling," Mason said. "Besides, it makes the bath all the more welcome. And you were beautiful undressing. A sight to behold. Don't you agree, old man?" he added, turning to Michael.

"Lovely. Stephen couldn't be more fortunate."

Mason laughed, but Dina didn't.

The script called for Stephen to discover Clarice in her bath, then to carry her off to bed where he makes passionate love with her. The bath sequences were shot quickly. And to Dina's relief, the water was reasonably warm. Mason used candlelight and shadow for subtlety.

Next they were to shoot Michael carrying her to the bed after a deep kiss. Mason wanted her dripping wet, and spent several minutes doing shots of water dripping from her arms and legs while the candlelight played on her slick skin.

By the time Michael was finally allowed to carry her to the bed, she was shivering violently. "Perfect," Mason said, after they'd cut.

"My teeth were chattering so hard I could barely say my lines," Dina protested.

"The effect was just what I wanted. You appeared frightened and cold. That's as it should be. Now Stephen is about to use his body to warm you, love. You crave not only him, but his body heat."

Michael had remained mostly silent, except when the camera was rolling. Out of necessity, Dina had related to "Stephen" and had yet to meet Michael's gaze when he was not in character. While the technicians got ready, Madhavi positioned Dina and Michael in the bed, laying a blanket over Dina for warmth until it was time to shoot the first sequence. As they lay there while the others were preoccupied, Michael spoke to her for the first time.

"I envy Stephen," he said softly. "I'd give anything in the world to be in his shoes."

"Isn't that a bit ironic, under the circumstances?" she replied.

"No, actually not. He has Clarice's heart, as well as her body. But you'll understand if I empathize with him a bit."

"It's only a movie, Michael."

"This isn't any easier for me than it is for you, though I'm sure for very different reasons."

Dina glanced toward Mason, who was in conversation with the gaffer and director of photography about the lighting. "This is our swan song, Michael. Let's do it with dignity. I'd like our last impressions of each other to be favorable."

"And memorable, I would hope."

"Just don't push it," she said.

"Isn't the tiniest part of you feeling nostalgic about me?"

"Not really." She clasped the blanket tightly to her throat. "Mostly I'm cold."

Michael began rubbing her arm and shoulder to warm her.

"Thanks," she said, "but I'm not that cold."

"You don't even want me to touch you? Dina, my sweet, in a matter of minutes we'll be making love."

"Clarice and Stephen. Not us."

"There's always the possibility we'll lose ourselves in it."

"*You* might," she snapped, hearing the defensiveness in her voice.

Mason came over to the bed and squatted down beside them. "How is everybody doing?"

"Let's get on with it, Mason," Dina said, more sharply than she intended. "I'm freezing."

"I know you're chilled, but try to relax, darling. I want to discuss this scene with you for a moment. I don't think a good, erotic sex scene can be choreographed. It's got to be spontaneous. The camera must see, but I don't want you making love for *it*. I want you making love for each other. I want you to be alone. I want you to forget anyone is here, including me."

Mason's words sent a tremor through her. Her instinct was to protest. He wouldn't say that if he knew what had been going on. He wouldn't even want Michael in the same room with her. Dina's teeth began to chatter.

Mason noticed her shivering. "Be a good chap, Michael, and warm the poor girl up, will you?"

Michael, who'd maintained a discreet few inches between them, moved closer, pressing against her. His warmth created mixed feelings. He rubbed her shoulder through the blanket and let his warm breath spill over her neck.

"This will be magnificent," Mason said, beaming. "Allow the cold to work for you, Dina. You need this man, and you also want him desperately."

She dropped her head back on the pillow and looked up at Michael. Fear of a sort Mason couldn't understand was raging in her heart. Michael was right. They were about to make love. And they would be doing it in front of her fiancé, with both his permission and encouragement. How could this be happening?

"All right," Mason said, moving back. "I'm going to roll the cameras, but remember, you are alone. Blanket, please."

The wardrobe assistant snatched it away.

"Camera . . . and . . . action!"

Dina was trembling when Michael moved his body partly over her. There was delight in his eyes, but also desire—that raw desire of his that she knew so well. He kissed her.

"'Clarice,'" he whispered. "'I want you so badly.'"

Her eyes were wide with awe. Michael drew his hand down her flank, making her shiver. He kissed her shoulder. She tentatively drew her fingertips across his cheek.

Dina was aware of the snowy evening, the drafty château, the candlelit bedchamber, the man in her bed, his warmth, his love—but everything else began to fade.

His touch incited her. She kissed him back fiercely, becoming deeply aroused. Seattle on a rainy night, the

Loire on a snowy evening, the firelight, the candle-light—it was all becoming one.

She began to feel a pulsing deep inside. Michael's fingers sank into her flesh. She started tearing at his clothes. He rose to his knees and removed his coat. The full-sleeved linen shirt he wore under it was open at the neck. She watched him remove it. Then he lowered himself so that the warm flesh of his chest pressed against the chilled nubs of her breasts. Her lips parted to accept his kiss.

Her body was soon on fire, the cold air of the château forgotten. All that existed was Stephen/Michael. She wanted him, needed him.

Michael kicked off his breeches so that they were both naked, their limbs entwined. She felt him press against her and she wanted him in her. Instinctively she opened her legs. Her breathing had become desperate.

He kissed her neck, drawing his tongue along her flesh. He kissed her breast, making her moan. "Oh, take me, Michael, please take me."

He pressed his body hard against her and kissed her, sinking his teeth into the flesh of her lips.

"Oh, Michael," she moaned.

"Cut!" The voice came over the rushing sound of their breathing.

It took a moment for Dina to realize what had happened. It was Mason, of course. She hadn't exactly forgotten him; she'd simply let him fade into the background. She'd been doing as he'd wished; she'd ignored his presence and lost herself in her desire.

He loomed up beside them, intruding into their love-making like an unwanted houseguest. "Dina," he said, an edge of sternness in his voice, "that was lovely, it truly was, but we must keep our lovers straight, mustn't we?"

She looked at him with perplexity. "What did I do?"

"You got Stephen confused with that celebrated film star who lives in L.A."

She shifted her eyes to the man in her arms. A smile crinkled at the corners of his eyes.

"You called me 'Michael,'" he said. "I think what Mason's suggesting is that Stephen would not be pleased."

Her mouth dropped open. "Oh, dear."

Michael eased himself off of her, pulling the sheet up over her. She clutched it to her throat, looking back and forth between them.

Mason didn't look hurt, nor even particularly upset. He looked as though one of his actors had bungled her lines, which was exactly what had happened. Michael was trying not to show emotion, but there was a hint of satisfaction on his face.

The horror of what had happened finally struck her. The reality of having all but had intercourse with Michael—on camera and with the world watching, not to mention calling him by his name—was too much to bear. She flushed, the color rising so fast in her cheeks that they began to burn. She felt as if the eyes of the world were on her.

"Most of the scene was perfect," Mason said. "You were both brilliant. We can work around the indiscretion. But I'd like to shoot some after-sex shots of your bodies and faces. Several close-ons and we'll call it a day."

Dina was so embarrassed, she couldn't speak. Even though she was practically comatose, she did her best while Mason took his "after-sex" shots. But he had to cajole her a little.

"That's a bit too terrified, love. Satisfaction is what we want. Contentment. This man has just given you the time of your life and you love him desperately."

She felt the tears well in her eyes. Mason mistook her humility and sorrow for other emotions. As soon as he'd gotten what he wanted he dismissed the crew. Dina quickly slipped into the robe the assistant brought her and sat for a moment on the edge of the bed, pondering what had happened.

Michael was dressing, too, but she didn't look at him. She was aware of Mason standing nearby. When she looked up at him, tears overflowed her lids and began running down her cheeks. He noticed.

"Dina, what's the matter?"

"Mason, I have to speak with you. In private."

The moment had come. She couldn't carry on with the charade any longer. The only way to put Michael behind her once and for all was to confess. She couldn't be sure how Mason would react in light of what he'd just witnessed, but she had to do it.

"We can step into the next room," he said, moving forward to take her hand.

Dina rose, glancing at Michael who, like her, was in a terry robe. Obviously he'd heard her. Maybe he knew what she was about to do, maybe he didn't. At this point she didn't care. Her life would be impossible unless she set things right with Mason.

Mason took her to a chair in the adjoining chamber and had her sit down. Then he stood waiting, his brow furrowed. "What is it, love?"

Dina drew a breath to fortify herself. She looked down at her folded hands. "Mason, I've been unfaithful to you," she said, the words nearly sticking in her throat. "I've agonized about this for weeks and I can't go on without confessing." She looked up at him, her eyes glistening. "I don't know whether you have it in your heart to forgive me, but I must tell you."

"Dina, what in God's name are you talking about?"

"I slept with Michael!" she blurted out. "In Seattle."

"What?"

She closed her eyes, drawing a ragged breath. "It was a terrible thing to do. I feel horrible about it. I've started to tell you a dozen times, my heart has been crying out to confess." She looked up at him. "I wouldn't blame you for hating me. You deserve better."

Mason was dumbstruck.

"Do you hate me?" she demanded.

"Darling, you've caught me totally by surprise." He shook his head as if to clear it. "I...I wasn't expecting anything like this."

"Michael and I have a past you aren't aware of. My mistake was in not telling you this before. We were more than friends, Mason. Michael and I were engaged. I came within a few days of marrying him."

"You're joking."

"No, it's true. Despite my love for you, Mason, I betrayed you. I failed you out of weakness, out of lust."

"That's not quite accurate." It was Michael, standing in the doorway, his hands in the pockets of his robe. "Dina didn't want to go to bed with me, Mason. I coerced her. I pressured her constantly for a month and finally caught her in a moment of weakness. It wasn't her fault, it was mine."

"Don't try to make excuses for me, Michael," she said.

"I'm not making excuses. I'm admitting defeat." He turned to Mason. "I love her," he said, "and I was hoping she still loved me. By hook and by crook I got her to bed, but I never got back her heart. I might have seduced the body, but that's as far as I got."

Dina lowered her eyes.

"I financed this film and I insisted on playing Stephen for one reason and one reason only—to have an excuse to be with her. I thought I'd be able to win her back. But I couldn't. She fought me every step of the way. I now see why. She loves you, not me."

When she looked up at him again, tears were rolling down her cheeks. Michael went over to her. He put his hand to her face affectionately, wiping away the tears with his thumb. "I would have traded all my successes—each accomplishment, every dollar I've ever made—to have won you back." He turned to Mason, offering his hand. "Treasure her," he said. "You have the greatest prize any man could hope to gain." Looking back and forth between them, he added, "I'm sorry to have put you through this. Maybe, in the long run, it will prove to be a service. Every relationship is strengthened when it's tested. I see now that my very best shot wasn't good enough."

Dina and Mason were both speechless. Michael went to the door.

"As soon as I'm packed, I'll be heading for Paris," he said. "Say goodbye to the rest of the cast and crew for me, Mason." He gave Dina a sad smile. "Break a leg, Geraldine Winterhalter. And be happy. You deserve the best."

He left her crying, with Mason standing helplessly by her side.

14

MICHAEL SAT IN THE front row, listening to a blond-haired woman reading her lines. She was doing a credible job, but she was not Desdemona. When she'd finished, he thanked her. She looked back at him uncertainly for a moment, then went over to the chair where she'd left her raincoat and umbrella.

His assistant director, Todd Macky, who'd been reading Othello's lines, sat down cross-legged on the stage, the script on his lap.

"We have your telephone number, don't we, Melissa?" Michael asked.

"Yes, sir."

"Good, we'll be in touch, then."

"Thank you."

He watched her move across the stage and down the steps. "Good night."

"Good night, Mr. Cross." She went up the aisle into the darkness at the rear of the empty theater. It wasn't until he heard the sound of the door closing that he knew she was gone.

Todd Macky hadn't moved. "What now, boss?"

Michael leaned back, slinging his arms over the backs of the adjoining seats. "We keep looking. If necessary, I'll bring someone in from New York. We've got to begin rehearsals next week at the latest."

"Time's getting short."

"Speaking of which, what time is it, anyway?"

"Almost seven," Todd said, looking at his watch.

"Get out of here, then. I've kept you late enough."

"Buy you a beer?"

"Thanks, no, Todd. I'm going home to look at some videotape of *Cold Hearts*."

"No rest for the weary."

"That's what they say."

Todd, a lanky fellow of thirty, got to his feet. He descended the stage, grabbing his coat from the aisle seat. "See you Monday morning?"

"Yeah, let's plan on finalizing everything but Desdemona, Todd. I may make some calls over the weekend, but I want the part cast by Wednesday. I'm going to spend three or four days in L.A., then back here, hell-bent for leather till opening night."

"It's the American way, I guess."

Michael smiled and waved as Macky made his way out of the theater. After the door had closed, Michael remained sitting there, staring at the empty stage.

It had been a dismal two weeks. He'd gone to his brother and sister-in-law's place in Indianapolis for Christmas. He'd played uncle with his two little nieces, signed autographs at their Christmas pageant, nearly spoiling it for the family, and caught a plane back to Seattle on the twenty-sixth. There was no going back to being an ordinary guy anymore, but that he could live with. Losing Dina—that last goodbye at Château Vaumas—had been the final blow. He would never be the same.

It was funny how he'd been guarding his feelings for her since their first breakup. Supposedly she'd been out of his life for good, but a part of him had refused to let go, even as they'd parted. It wasn't until he handed her over to Mason Fellows that he realized how he'd been clinging to his dream. The certainty he'd felt all along had been shattered at long last.

Wearily he got to his feet. He leaned on the stage in front of him, staring up at the blank wall in the shadows at the rear, remembering. In his mind he saw the Dina he'd first known in New York—young, impressionable, determined, in love. Then the Dina of their days in Seattle—soul mate and lover. And finally the Dina who'd been weak with desire, but hard of heart—first in that hotel room overlooking Puget Sound, then in a château in the snowy countryside of France. The Dina who would not allow herself to love him again.

His heart ached when he let himself think of what he'd lost. He ached with longing for her, and for their lost love.

At the sudden sound of footsteps, he spun around. A female figure was moving down the aisle, coming from the rear of the auditorium. He could see an umbrella in her hand. "Melissa?"

She didn't answer. It wasn't until she emerged into the light that he saw her face clearly. It was Dina. The sight of her made his heart stop.

Raindrops had spattered the front of her coat and speckled the black silk of her hair. Her eyes shone as she gazed at him. The drama of her entrance had made him speechless.

He touched her face, knowing more keenly than ever how it must feel to see a ghost, albeit in this case a beloved one. "I don't know what to say," he murmured.

"Not the Michael Cross I know—surely."

He took her hands and kissed them. Then he kissed her soft lips. "Tell me what happened. Why are you here?"

Dina took off her coat and tossed it on a seat. Then she leaned against the stage, beside him.

"It's Christmas Day. I'm in Southampton with Mason at his mother's house. There's an icy wind blowing in off the Atlantic. I'm watching it whip the bare tree branches outside the cottage. For the hundredth time in two weeks I think of you. And then I remember some lines you once recited to me. You said, 'I dream my dreams, for it is meant that I would dream them for us both.' Do you remember saying that, Michael?"

"It's vaguely familiar, but to be honest I don't remember the occasion."

"It was in my little loft, here in Seattle. You were making love to me. You'd recited some lines from Shakespeare, then you said those words. I don't know why they came to me, there in Southampton, but they did. In any case, everything suddenly became clear. I understood what you'd been doing for the past few months and I knew that I felt the same way. I realized you were dreaming for us both."

"Dare I say you're a slow learner, my love?"

"I knew I felt passion for you, Michael, but passion wasn't what I wanted most. I wanted a meaningful love. I wanted you to care for the right reasons. When you took the fall for me with Mason... When you sacrificed yourself... That was when I discovered you truly cared about me. Love is a willingness to give up what you want for the sake of the other person. You did that, Michael."

"If I'd known, I'd have thrown myself on the train tracks long ago."

"Maybe you had to discover that sort of love yourself."

He put his arm around her shoulder. "Maybe so. I know it wasn't easy walking away and leaving you with Mason. It may have been the hardest thing I've ever done."

"My heart went with you."

"Does that mean you'll be my Desdemona?"

"If you want me to be."

"What about Mason? Did you decide you don't love him, after all?"

"I cared for him. It was love, but not the sort for which you marry someone. I spent as much time trying to persuade myself of my feelings for Mason as I actually spent feeling them. With you I didn't have to try. When I let it come, the love was always there. Instantly."

He took her by the shoulders and folded her into his arms. "That wedding we called off, do we reschedule it for sooner or later?"

"I think later," she said. "I want to savor you a little while."

He kissed her tenderly on the lips. "I love you, Geraldine Winterhalter."

"And I love you, Michael."

They looked at each other with glistening eyes.

"You know, I've got a brand-new house in the pine trees with a great big fireplace and a wonderful soft carpet in front of it. Nobody's ever made love on it before."

"Are you making me an indecent proposal, Mr. Cross?"

"You can't expect me to be completely reformed in one night, can you?"

She laughed. "I suppose I have to allow you one vice."

"Thank God I picked the right one." He saw the love shining in her eyes and gave her another hug. He didn't want it to end. But then, he realized, it wouldn't. Not their love, not their wanting to be together. He let go of her and, taking her hand, said, "Come on, my love, let's go home."

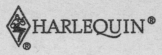

THE VENGEFUL GROOM
Sara Wood

Legend has it that those married in Eternity's chapel are destined for a lifetime of happiness. But happiness isn't what Giovanni wants from marriage—it's revenge!

Ten years ago, Tina's testimony sent Gio to prison—for a crime he didn't commit. *Now* he's back in Eternity and looking for a bride. *Now* Tina is about to learn just how ruthless and disturbingly sensual Gio's brand of vengeance can be.

THE VENGEFUL GROOM, available in October from Harlequin Presents, is the fifth book in Harlequin's new cross-line series, **WEDDINGS, INC.** Be sure to look for the sixth book, **EDGE OF ETERNITY,** by Jasmine Cresswell (Harlequin Intrigue #298), coming in November.

WED5

This September, discover the fun of falling in love with...

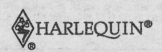

love and laughter

Harlequin is pleased to bring you this exciting new collection of three original short stories by bestselling authors!

ELISE TITLE
BARBARA BRETTON
LASS SMALL

LOVE AND LAUGHTER—sexy, romantic, fun stories guaranteed to tickle your funny bone and fuel your fantasies!

Available in September wherever
Harlequin books are sold.

◆ HARLEQUIN®

HARLEQUIN
Temptation
Lost Loves

RIGHT MAN...WRONG TIME

Remember that one man who turned your world upside down? Who made you experience all the ecstatic highs of passion and lows of loss and regret. What if you met him again?

If you missed any Lost Loves titles, here's your chance to order them:

Harlequin Temptation®—Lost Loves

#25589	THE RETURN OF CAINE O'HALLORAN by JoAnn Ross	$2.99	☐
#25593	WHAT MIGHT HAVE BEEN by Glenda Sanders	$2.99 U.S. $3.50 CAN.	☐ ☐
#25600	FORMS OF LOVE by Rita Clay Estrada	$2.99 U.S. $3.50 CAN.	☐ ☐
#25601	GOLD AND GLITTER by Gina Wilkins	$2.99 U.S. $3.50 CAN.	☐ ☐
#25605	EVEN COWBOYS GET THE BLUES by Carin Rafferty	$2.99 U.S. $3.50 CAN.	☐ ☐
	(limited quantities available on certain titles)		

TOTAL AMOUNT	$
POSTAGE & HANDLING	$
($1.00 for one book, 50¢ for each additional)	
APPLICABLE TAXES*	$_____
TOTAL PAYABLE	$_____
(check or money order—please do not send cash)	

To order, complete this form and send it, along with a check or money order for the total above, payable to Harlequin Books, to: **In the U.S.:** 3010 Walden Avenue, P.O. Box 9047, Buffalo, NY 14269-9047; **In Canada:** P.O. Box 613, Fort Erie, Ontario, L2A 5X3.

Name: _____

Address: _____ City: _____

State/Prov.: _____ Zip/Postal Code: _____

*New York residents remit applicable sales taxes.
Canadian residents remit applicable GST and provincial taxes.

LOSTF

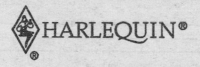

HARLEQUIN®

Don't miss these Harlequin favorites by some of our most distinguished authors!
And now you can receive a discount by ordering two or more titles!

HT #25525	THE PERFECT HUSBAND by Kristine Rolofson	$2.99	☐
HT #25554	LOVERS' SECRETS by Glenda Sanders	$2.99	☐
HP #11577	THE STONE PRINCESS by Robyn Donald	$2.99	☐
HP #11554	SECRET ADMIRER by Susan Napier	$2.99	☐
HR #03277	THE LADY AND THE TOMCAT by Bethany Campbell	$2.99	☐
HR #03283	FOREIGN AFFAIR by Eva Rutland	$2.99	☐
HS #70529	KEEPING CHRISTMAS by Marisa Carroll	$3.39	☐
HS #70578	THE LAST BUCCANEER by Lynn Erickson	$3.50	☐
HI #22256	THRICE FAMILIAR by Caroline Burnes	$2.99	☐
HI #22238	PRESUMED GUILTY by Tess Gerritsen	$2.99	☐
HAR #16496	OH, YOU BEAUTIFUL DOLL by Judith Arnold	$3.50	☐
HAR #16510	WED AGAIN by Elda Minger	$3.50	☐
HH #28719	RACHEL by Lynda Trent	$3.99	☐
HH #28795	PIECES OF SKY by Marianne Willman	$3.99	☐

Harlequin Promotional Titles

#97122	LINGERING SHADOWS by Penny Jordan	$5.99	☐
	(limited quantities available on certain titles)		

	AMOUNT	$
DEDUCT:	**10% DISCOUNT FOR 2+ BOOKS**	$
	POSTAGE & HANDLING	$
	($1.00 for one book, 50¢ for each additional)	
	APPLICABLE TAXES*	$_____
	TOTAL PAYABLE	$_____
	(check or money order—please do not send cash)	

To order, complete this form and send it, along with a check or money order for the total above, payable to Harlequin Books, to: **In the U.S.:** 3010 Walden Avenue, P.O. Box 9047, Buffalo, NY 14269-9047; **In Canada:** P.O. Box 613, Fort Erie, Ontario, L2A 5X3.

Name: _____

Address:_____City: _____

State/Prov.: _____ Zip/Postal Code: _____

*New York residents remit applicable sales taxes.
 Canadian residents remit applicable GST and provincial taxes..

HBACK-JS